THE
FIRST CYLINDER

THE
FIRST CYLINDER

A NOVEL
BY
JOSEPH DOUGHERTY

Cover art by Henrique Alvim Corrêa
Edited by David Bushman
Book design by Scott Ryan

Published in the USA by Fayetteville Mafia Press
Columbus, Ohio

Contact Information
Email: fayettevillemafiapress@gmail.com
Website: fayettevillemafiapress.com
Instagram: @fayettevillemafiapress
Twitter:@fmpbooks

ISBN: 9781949024548
eBook ISBN: 9781949024555

THE FIRST CYLINDER

Being an Unique, Contemporaneous, and Previously
Unpublished Perspective on the
Events Described in
Mr. H. G. Wells' *The War of the Worlds*
Presented Here in Unexpurgated Form for
the Enlightenment and Entertainment of the General Public

Scrupulously Translated From The Original Martian

BY

MR. JOSEPH DOUGHERTY

CONTENTS

"No one would have believed in the last years of the nineteenth century that this world was being watched keenly and closely by intelligences greater than man's and yet as mortal as his own . . .

. . . Yet across the gulf of space, minds that are to our minds as ours are to those of the beasts that perish, intellects vast and cool and unsympathetic, regarded this earth with envious eyes, and slowly and surely drew their plans against us."

—AN INTRODUCTION—

January 1, 1901

We at Wickwire and Pendergast prefer to let our authors and their works speak for themselves. We have never felt the need to intercede on behalf of such popular titles as "Practical Sanitary and Economic Cooking Adapted to Persons of Moderate and Small Means" by Claudine Marie Sperling, or "What Mrs. Henrietta Small Knows About Old Southern Cooking" by Mrs. Henrietta Small.

However, we would be less than honest with you and with ourselves if we failed to acknowledge that the particular work you now hold is unique in many respects and therefore might require a moment of preparation on the part of the reader.

Said reader does not need me to remind him that none of us faces the dawn of the new century with anything like the assumed confidence we held only a few short years ago. We assumed so much about the future, particularly that there was going to be one. With logic that now seems childish in the extreme we thought the future was in some way guaranteed. That it required no conscious thought or consideration on our part. The future would simply be there, waiting for us, appearing, solid and steady, as if by magic, just ahead of each step we took. A path waiting for our footfall. So we went through life, without ever looking down.

Times have changed.

What follows is the entirety of the manuscript Mr. J. Dougherty presented at our offices last summer. It includes the complete narrative as it was revealed to him along with a brief Afterword speaking to how this unprecedented document came to his hands.

That Mr. Dougherty should arrive at the doorstep of Wickwire and Pendergast with this work is an indication of the reversals and vicissitudes he has encountered along the way to its publication.

We are a small publishing house with a rather narrow purview. Up until now. Our most successful offerings to date have been cookery books. Most notably "The New Hampshire Housewife's Kitchen Compendium" by Mrs. Lavinia Godwin and "The Contemporary Hostess Prepares" by sisters Estelle and Regina Constable. Both of which you will find for sale at your local book merchant.

We are proud of what we do and the readers we serve, and feel no need to apologize for being a modest business with modest ambitions. We accept the fact that authors seeking a brighter spotlight and more aggressive sales will turn toward larger publishers. But in most cases the books of these writers tend to be the sort we would not be interested in reading, let alone publishing.

We have long accepted the fact that Wickwire and Pendergast is not the first port of call for the author seeking literary fame and fortune. Ours was clearly not the first door upon which Mr. Dougherty knocked when seeking a home for his book. To his credit, he made no secret of the fact that his work had been rejected promptly and with ill concealed contempt throughout not only Manhattan, but in Boston and Philadelphia as well.

He knew our catalog and recognized that what he was bringing to us was not typical of the works we usually present to the public. Not that his book was like anything anyone has ever encountered before.

Certainly there has been no shortage of books about the nightmare that so recently shrouded our world. Personal memoirs, military histories, scientific and political analysis, and certain questionable religious tracts make up the bulk of the titles. But there has been nothing, absolutely nothing like the bound pages Mr. Dougherty brought to us. No one had dared speak . . . or pretended to speak . . . for the demons who descended on this innocent planet without warning or mercy.

Clearly and on every level, publishing "The First Cylinder" would be a tremendous departure for us, a house known for "One Hundred Recipes for Pastry, Cakes, and Sweetmeats" by Dulcimer Thornhill, "Classic American Dainties and How to Prepare Them" by Portia Bigelow, and "Plain and Rich Cooking for New Brides" by Pamela Shoote Kernel. All of which, I feel obliged to mention, are available along with a host of other useful volumes from our imprint at your local book merchant or by prepaid mail order from our offices in Manhattan.

Complicating the decision even more was Mr. Dougherty's description of how the narrative came into his possession, details of which I will leave to his Afterword.

We are taking a risk by publishing this book, and the taking of risks is something this firm has assiduously avoided for the past seventy-one years. But to turn away from this challenge at this moment is something we have chosen not to do.

We are not where we were a short time ago. We are not who we were back then. We must acknowledge this or face extinction.

A final entreaty: the unusual turns of language, the foreign nature of the conversations reported here may challenge some readers. I urge you to give the chronicle a chance, to permit the unorthodox manner in which these strange creatures spoke, the thoughts they express, the life they describe, to find purchase in your mind and heart. I believe, for good or ill, you may find little separating us from those who would destroy us.

Mr. Remington K. Wickwire
Wickwire and Pendergast Publishers Ltd.
384 1/2 Lafayette Street
New York City, New York

For a printed copy of our entire catalog and a generous introductory offer, you are invited to send a self-addressed, stamped envelope to our offices. Attention: Miss Dinsmore.

Book One

The Coming of the Martians

I thought it hadn't worked. I thought we were still in the launching tube. Launching Tube. Right. It was a cannon. But cannon didn't sound right to Leadership. It carried the unfortunate connotation that we were being stuffed into a hole in the ground that was, more or less, pointed at the Earth. So they said the shafts punched into the plateau must be referred to as "Launching Tubes."

In any case, I thought we were still in the cannon, the launching tube. Still in the ground and they'd have to pull us out. I was asleep then I was awake and I thought it hadn't worked because it felt the same as when we were in the tube in the ground on the plateau.

All you could hear before the launch was the mewing of the cardos down in the larder and sometimes a loud clang when the cylinder hit the side of the launching tube as they lowered us in. We were each in our cells and we were sleepy from what they made us take to relax us before the concussion. I must have fallen asleep from what they gave us. I didn't remember hearing the cannon fire. Excuse me, the launching tube ignite. I asked around later and nobody else remembered hearing the explosion. That's why at first I thought it hadn't worked and they'd have to call the whole invasion off and, honestly, that would have been all right with me. None of this was my idea. We were all conscripted.

When I woke up I couldn't hear the cardos anymore. Turned out most of them were dead from the launch. Crushed and no good to anyone. We saved what we could, but everybody knew it wouldn't be enough to get us there. There was a buzzing in my head and that was the first time any of us knew Ddd was dead. Ddd was supposed to be in charge.

I heard some of the others saying, "Ddd is dead." "What are we supposed to do?"

Then someone told them to shut up. "We follow the plan. That's what we do. It's all automatic. At least till we get there. Then we'll do what they showed us how to do. It doesn't matter that Ddd is dead. We don't have to think about that. We don't have to think about anything. We were trained. All we have to do is do what we were trained to do and it will all work out. No thinking required."

"But the cardos are dead. Most of them. What are we supposed to do for food?"

"Shut up. Stop thinking."

So we all pretty much stopped thinking because, however you thought about it, it wasn't good. We were barely getting started and already it was messed up.

Somebody who wasn't Ddd told us to get out of the cells and drain what we could out of the dead cardos. I didn't know who said that, but it was something to do so we did it.

We put the dead Martians in vacuum bags and ran the crushed cardos through the pulp extractor.

The somebody who wasn't Ddd turned out to be Qqq and he took charge and we went along with it because at least there was someone in charge and it wasn't one of us. Qqq told us what to do and we did it.

So we got what we could out of the dead cardos and put it in canisters. Qqq said we'd use what we got from the dead cardos first before we fed off the last couple that were still alive. But we all knew that wouldn't be enough if it took as long to get there as they said it would.

We worked till we got tired then we crawled back into

the cells. The cells are small and round and not very deep. You have to fold your tentacles and crawl in head first till you're up against the back of the cell. Your body pretty much plugs up the entire cell so you're stuck there, your eyes up against the metal. I did that for a couple of cycles, but that particular kind of close darkness was getting to me. So I started backing into my cell. That way I could see out to the central shaft of the cylinder. The lights were always on in the shaft, but I didn't do much sleeping anyway. All you can do, squeezed in there like that, is try not to think.

You try not to think, but that doesn't work. Even if you don't think about where you are, you know where you are: In a tube in a cylinder getting thrown toward another planet. You try to tell yourself you're doing this for everyone back home so they'll have a better place to live, so everybody can get off Mars before it's too cold to do anything except curl up and die. But is this even going to work? Earth's not Mars. And it took so long to build the first fleet of cylinders. How are they supposed to build enough for everybody?

You sleep, you don't sleep. Sooner or later you feel the thrum of Qqq vibrating his tympano, letting you know it's time to get back to work which is mostly going over the invasion plans again and again. You grab the edge of the cell with your tentacles and pull yourself out and do what Qqq tells you to do. Nobody talks about what happened to Ddd. All we know is that Qqq found him dead after the launch.

Qqq found the spool with all the instructions so he knows as much as Ddd knew about the invasion; how we're supposed to put together the equipment and what we're supposed to do when we get there. Most of what we have is not in the best shape. Some of it's pretty beat-up.

I said this to Yyy and he asked me, "Why are you so negative about the invasion? You need to work on your enthusiasm. Enthusiasm makes the difference."

"Enthusiasm makes the difference, my friends," is what Qqq said when we were mopping up what was left of the dead cardos. Then he had it painted on the inside of the top of the cylinder, the part that's going to unscrew when we get there.

ENTHUSIASM MAKES THE DIFFERENCE!

That's the official motto of the invasion, "ENTHUSIASM MAKES THE DIFFERENCE." It's printed everywhere. All over the training facilities, the barracks, all over the surface transportation pods, on the pathways, in the shops. Where there isn't enough room to print the entire motto they print the acronym: EMTD. But nobody could figure out how to say it.

"If Qqq doesn't think you're enthusiastic enough, he could get the wrong idea about you," Yyy said to me.

I told Yyy I wasn't being negative I was only saying the stuff is old. Some of it isn't even proper military gear.

"That's not a proper tank," I said to Yyy when we were greasing the undercarriage of one of the tripods. "That's one of the harvesters they use to melt the ice caps in the winter."

"So?" Yyy said, then he dipped a couple of his tentacles in the lubricant and worked it into the joints where the upper sections screw in.

"So, I'm just saying, that's all."

"You better watch what you're saying, Vvv, is all I'm saying."

Somebody has to say something. Eventually. I mean, don't they?

"Those canisters," I said pointing at the rack of canisters some of the others were loading into a tripod hold. "You know what's in them? Nothing but the black smoke they use to kill the cufor when they want to clear the land for something. What are we supposed to do with that?"

"If it kills cufor it'll kill earthlings. You really need to work on your attitude, Vvv."

"It's hard to work on your attitude when you're stuck in a cylinder that stinks of dead cardos."

"What do you want Qqq to do? Unscrew the cylinder and shovel them out? Okay, it stinks, that's nobody's fault."

"Maybe if they'd strapped the cardos down or gave them a drug or something before the cannon was fired . . . "

"Launching tubes, Vvv. They're called launching tubes. You better be careful about your attitude or they'll start thinking you don't care how the invasion goes."

"Maybe I don't."

I was looking at the stack of canisters and the steam generators and when I turned back around Yyy was right in front of me and he hit me across the eyes with his dominant tentacle. That really hurts. You should never do that.

Then he grabbed my head between his tentacles and squeezed and I felt my head start to bulge at the top. Yyy pulled me close. I could see myself reflected in his eyes.

"You're stupid, Vvv," Yyy's words hissed past his lips. "It's bad enough you think the things you think, but the worst part is you saying them out loud. Nobody cares what you think, but they still might kill you for it. It's not like you can quit and walk home from here, Vvv. We're going to do this and we're going to be heroes and they'll name things after us. You're going to be a hero. A stupid hero, but a hero. And heroes don't ask questions."

•

My whole head hurt from the way Yyy squeezed it. It hadn't gone back to its proper shape by the time the next rest period came around and I had to squash myself to fit in my cell.

I don't want to be here. I want to be home. I don't want to invade anybody.

I want to be back in my skimmer on the Tirra Canal.

I want to be with my friends.

I want to play the crystals with them and make up songs.

It's not my fault Mars is dying. They should have done something about that a long time ago instead of expecting me to go off and invade places.

Old Zzz would sit in his swing across the path along the canal and complain about the noise we were making and how we were wasting our time, wasting our lives, and talk about how looking at us made him feel like a fool for conquering Venus. Did we think cardos sprout out of the ground? There wouldn't be any cardos if his generation hadn't fought the great wars. Old Zzz had no use for us. He cursed the day he and his brood ever pullulated such a thankless generation of buds.

As if any one of us ever asked to be budded.

•

"Tell me what it says there," Qqq pointed the tip of his dominant tentacle to the inside of the cap at the front of the cylinder. He had another tentacle around my head. He used it to pat my tympano. I think he thought he was being friendly. It came off as condescending.

I said what was written inside the cap.

"Enthusiasm makes the difference."

Yyy must have talked to Qqq about my lack of enthusiasm.

"Do you understand what that means?" Qqq asked me. He talked to me like I was a cercaria. It was insulting.

"It means things are different without enthusiasm."

"More than that, Vvv. A thing undertaken without enthusiasm is destined to fail. Can you understand that?"

"Yeah. I understand that." I didn't like Qqq when he was another cephalopod like the rest of us, but now that Ddd was dead and he was in charge I could see where I might end up hating him.

"Do you know why I wrote this on the inside of the cap?" Qqq asked me. He was tracing the edge of my tympano. Tapping it to emphasize certain words. I didn't want him touching my tympano.

"So we'd all see it. I guess."

"If that were so, I could have written it anywhere in the cylinder. But I didn't write it anywhere. I wrote it here, inside the cap. And I'll tell you why. I want the Martian chosen to unscrew the cap, the first Martian to see the new planet, I want him to be looking at those words as the cap is unscrewed and the cylinder opens. I want those words to vibrate within him as he greets the world we will conquer.

To be the first one out will be a great honor. History will begin with his action. For a time I thought I should be the first one out, as tribute to my dead friend Ddd. But I've changed my mind. The first Martian to touch the surface of Earth will be you, Vvv."

I don't need this.

"I'd just as soon not if it's all the same to you."
"It is not all the same to me, Vvv. Not at all the same, oh no. You lack enthusiasm, Vvv. And I don't want a Martian who lacks enthusiasm behind me in the line. I can't trust him, I can't depend on him. So, for the sake of all the others, all the brave and selfless entities on this ship who deserve better than to have an unenthusiastic coward behind them, you must be the first one up and out."
I think Qqq practiced this speech and was very happy with how he delivered it. I also wondered exactly what happened to Ddd while the rest of us were stuck, head first, in our cells.

•

Nobody was happy. We drained the last cardos and there was nothing left to eat. It became increasingly miserable in the cylinder. Work sleep work sleep work sleep and nobody was in a big hurry to crawl out of their cells when Qqq called us. Drifting along the central shaft, Qqq looked at me like it was all my fault, as if my lack of enthusiasm was spreading through the cylinder like a disease or something. I could tell from his expression how much he was waiting for us to get to Earth so he could shove me up the spout and off the cylinder.

Work rest work rest work rest work rest work rest.

I wondered if maybe we missed the Earth altogether. I wouldn't have been surprised. Considering how this whole invasion was thrown together as quick as it was. Leadership said this is how we're going to fix everything. We're going to do like we did with Venus and everybody knows the stories of Venus. The glorious victory over Venus. Leadership said it was time the current generation got a taste of the greatness that was Mars back then.

I thought for a while maybe they never even fired the other cannons when they saw us miss the Earth. No, they would have launched them anyway. Otherwise they'd have to say they'd made a mistake, they were wrong about something, and that wasn't going to happen.

Things were working out for Leadership. A couple of Opps spoke up when the invasion was proposed, but Leadership took care of that. Took care of them. Called them cowards who didn't have enough enthusiasm.

Enthusiasm Makes The Difference!

Some quick tribunals and suddenly the Opps got very quiet, and nobody had any problem with that. So Leadership went back to digging the holes for the launching tubes on the plateau.

If we missed the Earth no one back home would ever know. Leadership would come up with something heroic to say and figure out a way to blame the Opps. There are always some Opposites around when you need them. Even if you have to create them yourself.

Whatever happens, they'll tell everyone back home we died heroes. Dead heroes are the best kind. A dead hero is a very valuable commodity.

Rest work rest work rest work rest work.

•

I thought it was Qqq at first calling us out of the cells. But it wasn't Qqq vibrating our heads. It was the whole cylinder, shaking like someone had hit it with a big hammer. And when I got over that I realized it wasn't as cold as it had been up till then. It wasn't cold at all. It was warm. That wasn't a bad sensation. At least not at first.

"Martians, prepare!"

Now it was Qqq, floating up and down along the central shaft of the cylinder shouting at us, drumming on his tympano with his tentacles.

"Prepare for greatness!"

There really wasn't anything we had to do to prepare for greatness except push back into our cells as far as we could. The landing was supposed to be automatic. They called it a landing, but what they described didn't sound like a landing to me. It sounded more like falling until you hit something.

The warm feeling was getting more than warm.

The cylinder was spinning, I know that much. And shaking. Things began to come loose and started banging and rattling around inside the cylinder. All the metal started glowing red and the walls of the cell were too hot to touch, but there was no way to avoid touching them.

So, this is greatness, I thought as I watched Rrr bounce

around inside the cylinder. He'd been thrown out, or maybe he went crazy and crawled out of his cell, and now he was caroming all over the place. Hitting the sides of the cylinder, making a hissy sound with each hit and leaving little tendrils of smoke trailing after him as he angled off to hit someplace else.

"I don't like this!" Rrr yelled after the first couple of bounces. Then he didn't say anything. He kept bouncing and hissing and leaving strings of smoke to show where he'd been.

I closed my eyes. I couldn't breathe. The air was as hot as the walls of the cell and it hurt when you took it inside. I thought about how much everything was hurting and I thought really hard and I sent my thoughts to Mars. I hoped at least my thoughts would get home.

It was red behind my eyelids and then the red closed down to one small red point. A red dot. The way Mars must look from space. And that was that.

•

The first thing was the stink. One of the waste containers must have ruptured. As bad as it smelled before, it smelled worse then. I thought, *Is this what it smells like when you're dead?*

Next I realized we weren't moving. After all that time and all that distance, for the first time in what felt like forever we were motionless. It made sense that death and the lack of motion would go together. Then there was the weight. Not like there was a weight on top of me, but that the heaviness was me. All my insides were pulled down and I felt my head spread over the inside of the cell like it was filled with heavy mud. I could barely lift it and even when I did lift it I couldn't hold it up. I thought, *If this is death, I hope it doesn't last a long time.*

And we were crooked, tilted. All that time with no up and no down and now the whole cylinder was tilted with the cap at the up end.

"Report!"

Terrific. I was dead, but Qqq was dead with me.

We weren't dead. At least not all of us. So, I guess that made me lucky.

The lights came back on, but they didn't come on all the way and flickered when they did, which would have given me a headache if I didn't already have one from the heaviness. The dim light crawled around the cylinder as we worked to push ourselves out of our cells.

Poor Rrr was stuck to the wall. His face must have flattened against the bulkhead on his final bounce. He hung there, toward the cap end of the cylinder, his tentacles stretched out behind him. I was looking at him when there was this wet, stretchy sound and he slowly peeled away from the bulkhead, leaving his face behind, and tumbled down to the bottom of the cylinder.

Poor Rrr falling like that. Falling. Falling so fast. Gravity. There was gravity and lots of it. That's why we all felt so fat. We were hungry but we felt fat.

"Report! Answer! Respond!"

There were four of us left. Me, Qqq, Yyy, and Ppp. The rest of them were dead. Four left out of thirteen. You could see how this was going to work out. Qqq and Yyy had bonded over my lack of enthusiasm. That left me and Ppp to watch out for each other and Ppp wasn't even rated to run a tripod. Consider how stupid you'd have to be not to be able to get rated to run a tripod.

"Vvv! Your moment has come!" Qqq had developed the habit of speaking as if he was expecting someone to take down whatever he was saying. And he always looked like he was posing for someone to take an image of him while he was saying whatever momentous blather he was saying. I wish it had been Qqq who'd gotten his face melted onto the bulkhead.

Qqq and Yyy were on either side of the cap while I crawled my way up the length of the cylinder. I kept my eyes down. I didn't want to see the look on their faces as I pulled against all that gravity. Pulling up to get to the front end meant the cylinder crashed into Earth tail first.

Now, now, Vvv, don't say "crashed" say "landed." Where's your enthusiasm?

Qqq put one tentacle around my head and gestured to the inside of the cap with another.

"You are about to make history, Vvv," he said to me. "Your name will be added to the plaques. Canal bridges will be dedicated in your honor. Epic literature will be generated to assure your actions live long after you're gone. Buds will speak of you with awe and respect and admiration. I give you this, Vvv, and in that giving wash away the stains clinging to your lack of enthusiasm."

Yeah, I'm pretty sure Qqq killed Ddd when the rest of us were unconscious after launch. I think he thinks I think that's what happened and that's why he was sending me up the spout. Dead heroes can solve a lot of problems.

I couldn't look at Qqq anymore so I turned away and looked at the inside of the cap.

¡ƎƆNƎꓤƎℲℲIꓷ ƎHꓕ SƎꓘAM MSAISΩHꓕNƎ

What a great way to start an invasion: Backwards and upside down.

I wrapped my tentacles around the grips at either side of the cap and started to twist it. There was resistance, but not as much as I thought there'd be. Maybe the fall knocked it loose. Two tugs and the cap was turning. Behind me I heard Qqq and Yyy moving back. Whatever was out there, the glory would be all mine.

It was hard at first, then easier. I turned the cap, slowly rotating the motto in front of me. It went around once. It went around again. It went around a third time. I remember watching them screw the cap in place before they lifted us into the cannon. It was a long time screwing us in. Turning and turning, like they were shutting us up in an urn. It was going to be a long time unscrewing it.

I lost count how many times the words turned around in front of me. I lost track of how long it was taking me to unscrew the cap. I thought about stopping, but then I'd have to start again so I kept turning. I was listening. I don't know what I expected to hear, but all I could hear was the metal sliding against itself. I guess I thought I might hear something from outside, but that wasn't going to happen. I wasn't going to get a hint about what was out there until the cap was all the way unscrewed.

Watching Qqq's motto turn around and around I realized exactly how stupid we'd all been. How nobody ever asked the one question we should have asked about the cylinders: How were we supposed to get home in them?

Whatever was going to happen out there, once I got the damn cap off, the one thing that would never happen, was screwing the cap back on so we could leave for home. None of us had ever asked how we were going to get home after the invasion.

Which means, I guess, Qqq was right. Enthusiasm does make the difference. It keeps you from examining exactly what they're doing to you.

And that's what I was thinking when I twisted the cap clear of those last few threads and it rattled off the end of the cylinder nearly taking me with it. I let go of the grips and pulled back my tentacles and listened to the cap fall into what I figured was soft dirt next to the cylinder.

There was a rush of air all around me as the rank atmosphere inside the cylinder mixed with whatever the bubble around the Earth is made of. It blew over me and condensed on my skin.

I held my breath after the cap fell. I didn't know what was out there and, honestly, I wasn't curious. Eventually I had to exhale and take a breath of what the air was like.

I thought it was poison. It was so much thicker. No, not thicker. There was so much more of it than I was used to. There were smells in the Earth air. Smells I didn't recognize, but better smells than what was behind me in the cylinder.

There was something sweet in the air and something like the smell you get sometimes coming off the cardos when you hold them down and slide the pipette in them. It comes off their skins.

I took another breath. Bigger this time. Deeper. And the air filled my head, filled my body and I felt dizzy for a moment. That's when I figured it might have poison in it and I better say goodbye. But it wasn't poison. It was serious stuff, but it wasn't poison. It was . . . Life. I don't know how else to say it. It was something filling me up. I could feel it pushing into my lungs and through my heart and out to every part of me, all the way out to the tips of my tentacles. They started to tingle, as if they were surprised to feel the way they did.

How could air be so different?

Behind me in the tunnel leading to the cap I could hear Qqq and Yyy letting out little squealy noises when they got their first breaths of the Earth air pouring into the cylinder, washing over us.

And I heard them differently. I heard them louder, clearer. As if the air had tightened my tympano, made it more sensitive to every sound.

And there were sounds coming in from outside, pouring down on us. A sound like sand on metal; scoops of sand being sifted down on a thin sheet of metal. Other sounds. Sort of animal sounds. Like the sounds that come from the cardo pens sometimes. Vocalizations that don't mean anything but sometimes at night you can convince yourself they're speech.

"Don't just squat there. Take a look outside," Qqq barked

and slapped the back of my head with a tentacle. The air was making me feel like I could turn around and bite Qqq's tentacle off at the base.

Above me the sky was a color I'd never seen in the sky before. Not in the real sky. I saw something like it once. It was winter and the tripods had been melting parts of the ice caps and the canals were running fast and deep. I was sitting on the bottom of the canal. I did that when I wanted to think. I looked up through the water moving past me, up toward the sky. The sky through the water was dark blue. I know the sky wasn't blue, the sky is never blue, but all the water between my eyes and the surface of the canal was bending the light, pushing it into a different color.

That's something like what I saw when I looked up. A circle of dark, dark blue shot with stars far beyond the mouth of the cylinder. Maybe I was looking at Mars. Probably not. But it hurt to think I was looking at home.

"Go up! Look around! Make a preliminary report!"

So, I crawled forward. Not because I wanted to see what was out there, but because I wanted to get away from Qqq.

I pulled myself up and out until my eyes were above the lip of the cylinder.

The sound of sand on metal was louder now and I could see where it was coming from.

The sky was not as dark closer to the ground. I looked behind me and I saw the last bit of a boiling big sun, much bigger than I'd ever seen the sun, slipping behind this choppy row of some kind of stalks. The horizon looked farther away than it does on Mars. But the sun. If it looked that bright at sunset, what's it going to be like during the day?

There were more of those stalks closer to us. Tall stalks growing out of the ground and crowned with something like balls of shredded scroll. I could see the shredded bits moving as the sun disappeared. The noise I was hearing was coming from the shredded scroll. The air was moving, but there wasn't what you'd call a wind. The wind at home is mean and hard, but this was something softer. It was still moving air, but it wasn't a punishment like at home. And this slow, soft air moving around the shredded scroll, rubbing it together, that was the noise I heard that I thought was sand on metal. I thought it was a very pleasant sound.

The stalks with the balls of shredded scroll were all around the field we were in. The field wasn't dirt except where we scraped it on the way in. There was something covering the ground, a short green substance I thought must be a kind of vegetation. The wind was moving that, too. It was cool and I closed my eyes and listened to the song coming from the field. Maybe this place wouldn't be so bad after all.

"Report! Report! Report!"

However nice a place this turned out to be it would be less nice as long as Qqq was in it.

I opened my eyes and looked around. That's when the animal noises started getting louder, more distinct, and I saw the figures around us. They looked like cardos standing on their hind appendages. But their heads were really, really small. How could a head that small keep an animal alive? And there was something wrong with their skin. It was all rumpled and hanging around them. There were dozens of these Earth cardo. Keeping their distance. For the moment.

I could see some other animals, bigger than the Earth cardos. They reminded me of thoats, but with four appendages, not the normal eight. They were attached to spindly boxes that weren't sitting on the ground but were propped up on sets of large rings. Four rings for each spindly box.

"Report at once, Vvv!"

I started to turn around to shout back down at Qqq that if he was in such a hurry to know where we were he should crawl up, stick his own big head out of the cylinder, and take a good look for himself. That's when I fell out of the cylinder and onto the dirt that was all pushed up around us like a trench, sort of a pit.

Well, I bet that impressed the cardos, I told myself as I was trying to get my tentacles untangled. First Martian on Earth and he falls on his face in the dirt. Really great, Vvv.

Then I saw I wasn't alone. Something moved a couple of spans away from me. One of the Earth cardos was trying to claw its way out of the pit that formed when we landed, but the dirt was too loose and it was too scared and the more it scrambled the more it slid back down. It made noises while it was doing this. They sounded more like a whimper than the mew cardos usually make.

It was pretty close so I got a good look at it. As I said, like a cardo but with a tiny head. Skinnier. Like something all put together out of sticks. And it wasn't skin that was hanging from it. It was a kind of wrapping. Different parts of it were wrapped in pieces of what I guessed was cloth. It looked like the fabric they use to make the sails for skimmers.

It was mostly covered with this fabric. I guess they pick up the pieces they like and wrap it around them. Maybe it was how they tell each other apart.

Cardos all look the same, except there are two distinct varieties. You need one of each if you want to make more. I knew someone who did that for a living, breed cardos. He told me what was involved in getting them to reproduce. It sounded pretty disgusting.

There was this moaning sound coming from beyond the crest of the dirt. I looked toward the sound, toward the cardos in the field, all wrapped in different bits of fabric. I saw they were all backing away. What they were backing away from was Yyy sneaking a look over the lip of the cylinder. Qqq must have shoved him up after he saw me fall. Yyy was shaking all over. He had something in his non-dominant tentacle. I couldn't see what it was.

"Are you all right, Vvv?" his voice was trembling as much as his body.

"I think so."

"What happened? You were there, then you weren't there."

"I fell out."

Yyy's eyes grew till they were almost touching in the middle, taking up most of his face.

"WHAT'S THAT?"

He was pointing at something behind me. He was pointing at the scared Earth cardo that was trying to claw its way out of the hole.

"I think it's something like a cardo. Their heads are really small . . . " I started to tell him, but he was out of the cylinder when he heard the word cardo, tossing himself down on his tentacles that folded under him because of how heavy we all felt.

He bumped past me and that's when I saw what he was holding. He was holding a pipette. He must have grabbed it on his way up, something he thought he could use as a weapon. Yyy was headed toward the beast, kicking up dirt and sand as he tried to figure out how to walk on this planet. He looked like an idiot.

The Earth cardo saw him coming and started to make a noise like "Gawd, Gawd, Gawd," and tried even harder, and less effectively, to pull itself over the edge to freedom. Yyy was tossing himself at the stick figure in the dirt and finally grabbed hold of it with his tentacles and flipped the frightened animal over on its back.

I yelled at Yyy to stop. Actually all I could manage to yell was "Hey!"

Yyy put one tentacle across the thing's throat then shoved the pipette through the rags and into its thorax. That's not how you feed from a cardo, that's how you kill them. Yyy didn't care. He was hungry. Yeah, well, so were the rest of us.

Bright red gushed out of the end of the pipette. It must have been blood, but it was much more red than any blood I'd ever seen. It shot up like a sticky geyser and splashed against the side of the cylinder. The shell was still hot and the blood sizzled and smoked where it hit the skin of the cylinder.

Then Yyy closed his lips over the end of the pipette and started sucking. The cardo was kicking under Yyy. I could see one arm of the thing, not flapping, but making wavy circles.

Cardos don't have tentacles. Their upper limbs are like tentacles, but not as flexible. That's because they have this weird armature of hard material under the surface of their skin. It keeps them upright. The upper limbs end in clusters of flesh wrapped around tiny hard rods that bend on hinges. They can hold objects with these projections. I think the technical term is pseudotentare. Most call them pseudos. They're like stubby little tentacles at the end of each appendage. Five of them on each upper limb. There are even more primitive attempts at articulation at the ends of their hind appendages. The ones down there are completely useless.

The kicking and waving stopped, but Yyy kept sucking on the pipette. Sucking the dead thing dry. I moved back, part way under the end of the cylinder. I knew what was going to happen next.

Yyy's whole body heaved peristaltically and he pushed back from drinking, leaving the pipette still in the cardo's chest.

Yyy opened his mouth and let out a gross gagging noise. He retched once without producing anything then he heaved again and all that blood came gushing back out, spraying everywhere. The hot blood smelled like iron.

"What is going on out there?"

I looked up and saw Qqq at the lip of the cylinder. He didn't look very enthusiastic.

"Yyy drank an Earth cardo. It made him sick," I said.

"Are they poison?" Qqq demanded.

"I don't think so," I said. Like I'd know. "He overdid it. He was hungry and he saw food and there's your result."

Then I saw the cone in Qqq's tentacle. He was coming

out to take an image. Maybe we were supposed to take the cone and record an image of him heroically stepping on to the new world. Except the pit was a mess, everything covered with blood, Yyy groaning in the corner, rubbing himself, trying to wipe the blood from his face, the dead Earth cardo with the pipette sticking out of it. Yeah, let's all take an image to make everyone back home proud of us.

"What are those?"

Qqq was looking out over the edge of the pit, to the field and the scroll stalks. I crawled up and looked. I could see figures moving around out in the last light. Moving between the stalks, hiding, but still watching, surrounding the cylinder in a rough oval of animal motion.

"Earth cardos," I said.

"There are a lot of them," Qqq whispered. "Too many. They might overwhelm us. We can't allow ourselves to be overwhelmed!"

I went over to Yyy and asked him if he was okay or if he was going to be sick again.

"I think I'm okay," he said.

"What do they taste like?" I asked him.

He opened and closed his mouth a couple of times, his lips making a popping noise.

"Sort of like cardo," he said. "But they taste more like metal than regular cardos."

"That's what I figured, from the smell."

"Pretty rich stuff. But I think I can get used to it."

"We better."

Qqq was still at the mouth of the cylinder, posing for a statue.

"What we need to do is secure and maintain a perimeter. Yes, that's what we need. A good, solid perimeter."

"Maybe some weapons," I said. Qqq was right about there being enough cardos to cause a problem if they stampeded.

"That was going to be my next priority," Qqq said. Sure it was. "Vvv, bring out the helio, we have to let Mars know we're here and in charge. Yyy, clean your face and break out the portable convector. We've got a perimeter to secure."

I helped Yyy climb back into the cylinder. That close, I could smell the blood all over him. It made me hungry.

•

We took the dead Martians outside, crossed them with the distillate, burned them, and read from the scrolls before we scattered the ashes. We threw the pulp from the extractor and the dead Earth cardo over the rim of the pit.

Ppp was the only one of the four of us who hadn't been out of the cylinder so I made him come with me when I took the helio outside. We set it up on the stand so the dish was above the cylinder then turned it to the sky and listened.

I was surprised that we actually heard from some of the other cylinders. They would start arriving soon.

"So, we won't be here alone, right?" Ppp asked me.

I wasn't paying too much attention to him. I was thinking about the idea of all those cardos wandering around with no keepers.

"Right, yeah," I finally said to him. "We won't be alone. There'll be others. Lots of others."

I must have made Ppp nervous the way I was straining to look over the edge, to get a sense of how many cardos there were.

"Other cardos?"

"I don't know. Maybe."

"What if it's not cardos coming, but something else?" he asked me. "We're in charge of the cardos at home. Who's in charge of the cardos here? Who feeds on them?"

"We're going to feed on them. We'll come here to live and we'll eat the cardos." I felt bad telling Ppp this. It wasn't a lie, but I made it sound easy and I didn't think it was going to be as easy as they told us it would be. Nothing ever is.

"But doesn't there have to be someone here eating the cardos already? The place can't be all cardos, running wild. Somebody here eats the cardos. What do we do when we meet them?"

"You've been thinking about this, haven't you?"

"I try not to, but . . . yeah, I thought about it."

Thinking, I could tell, was something Ppp didn't enjoy. He didn't have much practice with it and hadn't mastered the mechanics of the process. So he was left with all these questions colliding in his head. Poor bud.

But he had a point. Who was eating the cardos before we showed up?

The colors were all gone from the sky. We turned on the work lights and helped Yyy unload the portable convector.

•

Qqq sent a message on the helio to the other cylinders. He told them about the crash . . . I'm sorry, the landing . . . and how there were four of us left but we were in good spirits and ready to face the enemy. The cylinders en route were supposed to relay the message back to Mars, but no one was sure the messages would get all the way home.

I'm telling you, I don't think a great deal of planning went into this enterprise.

We watched the Earth's one moon come up and we weren't ready for that. It's larger than Phobos and Deimos put together. It has the same kind of pockmarks on it, but the edges are much smoother. Not lumpy at all. It's white and clean and bright. Phobos and Deimos look like dirty rocks by the side of a road compared to this moon.

"What's that over there?" Yyy was pointing at something in the moonlight.

There was a cluster of cardos moving out from behind a stand of scroll stalks and walking toward the cylinder. It was hard to see how many, maybe ten or so.

"The one at the front. What's it got in its pseudo?" Qqq demanded.

The one in the lead was holding a long stick above the group and at the end of the stick was a white rag that moved in the gentle breeze.

"I think it's a weapon," Yyy said.

"I think it's a stick," I said.

"Why would you tie a rag around a stick?" Yyy said.

"Why would you tie a rag around a weapon?" I said.

"Stick or weapon, weapon or stick, we must maintain a secure perimeter and that's what we're going to do," Qqq said. "Elevate the convector!"

We cranked the convector until the oculus and chamber were above the cylinder so it had a clear view of the entire field.

"They're still coming. What should we do?" Ppp said. He was starting to shake.

"We'll brush them back a little and see what happens," Qqq said. He wasn't shaking, but his voice was. "Prime the convector!"

The convectors on the tripods are linked to the power plant, but this small unit runs from a portable energy source. Ppp and I got on either side of the convector while Yyy grabbed the loop at the end of the cord threaded into the recoiler and gave it a pull.

The spring groaned as the recoiler yanked the cord out of Yyy's tentacle. The convector coughed and belched three times before it stalled, sending a luminous cloud of green smoke above us. The smoke glowed long enough and floated high enough for us to see the faces of the cardos coming toward us. They must have been frightened by the smoke because they stopped their advance across the flat vegetation between us and the stalks.

When Yyy saw the look on their tiny faces he laughed a snort of a laugh.

"Pull the cord," I told him.

He grabbed the cord with his tentacle and gave it a serious yank. This time it caught. There was another belch of smoke then the bleed from the chamber was clean and it started to charge.

"Now what?" Yyy called up to Qqq.

Qqq waved the tip of his dominant tentacle toward the group led by the cardo holding the stick with the white rag.

"Brush them back," he said. "Do I have to tell you how to do everything? Point it at the ground and brush them back."

Yyy put his eye to the range finder and moved the levers. Then he looked at me and said, "Push the button."

So, I pushed the button.

We felt the static charge crackling all over us. Then the hum of the apparatus engaging, the soft glow of the oculus. Then the screaming started.

Qqq was at the rim and saw it happen.

He looked back, saliva flying from his lips, and yelled at us.

"What did you DO?"

Yyy scrambled up the dirt to reach Qqq. I was right behind him. When I looked back Ppp was trying to crawl under the cylinder, covering his tympano with his tentacles.

I got to the edge and looked out under the ray from the convector as it rippled the air above me. I followed the path of the beam to where the group of cardos was on fire. The rag on the stick burned like a torch for an instant then it crumpled to the ground. The cardos were trying to cover themselves, trying to scrape the fire off, but the fire wasn't on them. They were the fire.

"What did you DO?"

Yyy's face was blank. All eyes and a mouth, but no expression.

"I was aiming at the vegetation," he said.

The group of cardos was separating and stumbling away in all directions, falling down and beating the ground, rolling and screaming. Then they stopped moving and continued to burn.

"Turn it off! Turn it off!" Qqq ordered, pointing at the convector.

"It has to cycle," Yyy told him.

"Well, point it away from them, do that, can't you?"

"Yeah. I can do that."

Yyy stumbled back down to the controls of the convector and put his eye to the range finder. He moved the levers again. Qqq and I watched as the beam shifted from its original position, dragging flame behind it as it moved across the vegetation. But there were Earth cardos all over the field. Everywhere Yyy moved the beam there were dozens of them and the convector touched them off. They burned like sticks. Like screaming sticks.

Yyy tried to lift his sights. The beam touched the scroll stalks and they exploded with dull thuds, one after another. Everything was burning. Orange and yellow and white flames everywhere lighting up the bottom of the smoke climbing into the sky, covering the moon. The convector swept a good hundred degrees before the discharge sputtered and stopped.

"Crank it down! Crank it down!" Qqq slid with the dirt to the bottom of the pit.

Yyy and I cranked the head of the convector below the rim.

You could hear the cardos making noise and running and you could hear the stalks burning and exploding. The wind changed and pushed the smoke over us. The three of us were gathered around the base of the convector. Three of us?

I looked around for Ppp. I saw him, jammed against the underside of the cylinder where it pushed into the ground. His eyes were small and swimming with darkness. And he had jammed all his tentacles into his mouth. He was drooling and whimpering and trying to get further under the cylinder.

"How am I going to explain this?" Qqq moaned.

That was the status of things. Qqq afraid he was going to be blamed for something, Ppp whimpering and drooling, Yyy under the convector afraid Qqq was going to pin all this on him. And me, feeling as sick as Yyy must have felt after he drank all that blood.

Above us, the metal case surrounding the hot convector elements started to click and snap as it cooled.

It was in this fashion the Martian invasion of the planet Earth began.

•

I don't know how long we sat there feeling sorry for ourselves. All around us was the fire, still burning through the scroll stalks, making the underside of the smoke flicker orange. Maybe we were waiting for the fire to die down, but it never really did. Finally, and I honestly have to say to his credit, Yyy made a suggestion.

"Maybe we should report in," he said. "Somebody is going to want us to report."

Then he looked at Qqq. Qqq looked at us.

"What am I supposed to tell them?" he said, gesturing one tentacle toward the smoke and flames.

If I didn't say something, Yyy would say something and the way Qqq was acting, I didn't want Yyy to get any kind of edge over me.

So, I got up as much as I could on my tentacles and looked at Qqq.

"Tell them it's going well," I said.

The others were quiet. They looked at me like they expected me to say something else. They didn't know I was making it all up as I said it.

"What?" Qqq asked, his head tilted to one side which was either because he was thinking or he was tired of holding his head up.

"Tell them we were attacked by Earth creatures, but we were able to repel their forces," I said.

"What forces?" Yyy said. "They were a bunch of cardos."

"They must have belonged to somebody," Qqq fretted. "That means we destroyed somebody's property."

I moved to put myself between Qqq and Yyy.

"Really, Qqq," I started with something that could have been a smile on my face if he wanted to see it that way. "Did you think we were going to invade a planet and not break something in the process?"

"But nobody told us to kill anything," Qqq said, nervously balling up the ends of his tentacles. "We were supposed to wait for orders. Then, when the other cylinders landed, we were going to move as one inexorable force."

Qqq might have been afraid of the danger we were in, but he was more afraid of getting in trouble with the entities in charge of this circus. My job was to help him ditch responsibility while looking good up the chain of command. Once he was confident of that, we could concentrate on not getting ourselves killed. An event, I believed, with a high order of probability.

"What could they expect us to do?" I asked him. "Sit here and be overwhelmed? You said yourself you didn't want us to be overwhelmed."

"Yes, I did."

I pointed at him with my dominant tentacle.

"And that, Qqq, was the right decision."

"Yes, it was, wasn't it?"

I almost had him.

"You bet it was," I told him. "What's important now is to make sure we put events in the proper context. There's no reason we shouldn't look good coming out of this. It's all about how we describe it. You can report we set fire to someone's cattle, or you can report we faced our alien foe with bravery and enthusiasm."

I could tell Qqq was listening to me, but also thinking about what I was saying. He was looking past me, putting it together in his head. When he finally looked at me again, I could tell he was looking at me differently. Up until then Qqq thought I was someone he couldn't trust. Now he was starting to think of me as somebody who could help him get what he wanted. A change of attitude like that could help keep us alive a little while longer. Qqq wanted to be a big deal coming out of this. Me, all I wanted was to get out of it in one piece.

Yyy must have seen what I saw on Qqq's face because he decided it might do him some good if he backed me up.

"Maybe Vvv is right," he said, putting one tentative tentacle tip on the side of my head. "It was a bunch of cardos, but nobody knows that except us."

"What if they weren't cardos?"

We all turned to the voice. It was Ppp. He was still wedged under the cylinder, but he'd taken his tentacles out of his mouth and he wasn't shaking anymore.

"What are you talking about?" Yyy demanded. "Of course they were cardos. You saw them yourself."

"I'm thinking maybe they weren't cardos like we're used to." Ppp's voice became stronger the more he spoke. "I've never seen cardos that decorated themselves like that, with that cloth, and some of them had things on the tops of their heads. I never saw anything like that before."

Ppp was crawling out from under the cylinder now. Yyy moved to stand in his way. He didn't want him getting too close to Qqq.

"What exactly are you trying to tell us?" Yyy demanded.

I thought Ppp was going to crawl back under the cylinder, but he didn't. He drew himself up as much as he could and looked straight at Yyy.

"I'm saying they could be the highest form of life on this planet and we wouldn't know it."

"That's crazy," Yyy flicked his dominant tentacle to dismiss the whole idea. "You saw them."

"Just because they don't look like us doesn't mean they're not as smart as us." Ppp said.

That thought hung in the smoky air for a while. I didn't know about Yyy and Qqq, but there was something about Ppp's suggestion that made me nervous.

I tried to shake off this queasy feeling. Even if Ppp was right, which he probably wasn't, and those rag-covered cardos were the highest form of life, we might still be in pretty good shape going forward. We were supposed to demoralize the native population and it seemed to me we'd made a pretty good start on that job.

"We should assemble one of the tripods," Qqq had been sitting there thinking, too. But he wasn't thinking about what were the smartest creatures on the planet, he was thinking about making sure we all looked good when the other cylinders started to arrive.

•

The sun came up and the sky went from black to gray to yellow to orange to blue. Not the same blue I saw when I first opened the cylinder. This was a shiny, fired blue. Like the tiles from the old cities where the ones with the golden eyes were supposed to have lived. They used to let you go up there, way up in the Ylla Mountains, to look for chips of blue and red and green and yellow tile. Now they don't let anybody go up there. They haven't for a long time.

And this blue sky was crowded with big whipped blobs of something moving, drifting, the way foam floats on the canals. I blinked when I realized what those blobs must be made of: Water vapor.

I'd heard that's what Martian skies once looked like, a long time ago when there was enough heat to warm the surface of the canals and enough atmosphere to hold the vapor close to the ground. But those were remembered as thin, stringy things; pale worms in the sky. These blobs were tremendous, undulating forms, moving in a slow promenade. Water, in the sky. I wondered how they got it down when they needed it.

"What are you looking at?"

I lowered my head. Yyy was on the other end of the tripod tread we were unloading.

"Nothing," I said. Which, in a way, was true.

They trained us how to put together the tripods when we were on Mars, but everything is heavier here so it took longer to drag the segments out of the cylinder. To put them together you followed the diagrams. The diagrams didn't have glyphics on them, they had drawings of how the parts were supposed to fit together and how you twisted them a certain way to lock them in place or how you were supposed to bolt them or screw them. I think they designed these things to be put together by anyone no matter how stupid they were. We were supposed to call them War Machines, but everybody knew they were the harvesters sent to the ice caps every winter to melt enough water for the year.

A fits into B that attaches to C and slips down over D.

Since it was the four of us we decided to put together one War Machine. There wasn't anybody left alive to operate the others. They're designed to carry three, but we figured we could all fit under the cowling. The plan was to have the tripod finished by the time it got dark, start off, and find the second cylinder, which should be down by then. Qqq wants to make a big show out of being there when they unscrew the lid.

Working was supposed to take our minds off how hungry we were. It didn't. Of course, Yyy didn't have that problem. He was still belching metal-smelling belches from the blood he managed to suck out of the cardo before he made himself sick. The rest of us couldn't remember the last time we had something to eat. We looked at the burnt cardos in the field, but there was nothing left of them to salvage.

Halfway through the day, we got lucky with that aspect of the situation.

•

We got the tripod up on the second set of articulated riser segments and had started loading in the gas canisters and the other gear when we took a break because of how hot it was getting. Not hot like when we crashed, but hot.

The sun here is bigger, much bigger. It hurts to look at it. I wondered if it's like this all the time. It was hot and my eyes hurt so I slipped into the shade under the cylinder to rest. Yyy was inside with Qqq, who was working on what he wanted to put in the report of our first pitched battle with the Earth cardos. I suggested we don't call them Earth cardos, but call them Earth creatures. I thought it sounded more formidable. Qqq liked the idea. I looked over at Yyy when Qqq said that. Yyy wasn't happy Qqq liked my idea. Ppp had done more than his share of moving equipment from the cylinder to the tripod and was asleep.

I was alone outside the cylinder when what happened next happened.

I closed my eyes and was listening to all the noises this place makes. Listened to the air moving what was left of the scroll stalks, and other sounds. Trilling sorts of sounds. And buzzing. I was starting to suspect at least some of those sounds were coming from living things.

When I opened my eyes I was looking up at the ridge of dirt surrounding the cylinder. There I saw a little round bump with a rag attached to the top of it.

It was an Earth cardo looking over the edge of the dirt, staring at the tripod. I guessed it hadn't seen me there in the shade, otherwise it wouldn't have been so bold.

And I knew right then I owed Yyy an apology for how I felt about the way he acted the night before when he saw that cardo trying to scramble out of the hole. I knew exactly what he felt when he saw his first meal in such a long time.

At least I didn't go crazy and scramble to catch the thing. I figured out how to do it right and not take the chance of it getting away.

I snapped my dominant tentacle as far as I could extend it and wrapped the end around the cardo's neck. Then I yanked him over the edge and called to the others inside the cylinder.

The cardo was getting over the surprise of being pulled into the pit and started to struggle. I tightened the tentacle around its neck a little and it stopped struggling. Mostly. There was a sound from the other side of the piled up dirt. Two other cardos. I think they were calling to the one I was holding.

"Chaalee. Chaalee. Yoollal ri."

"Chaalee may te."

The one I was holding looked like he was trying to call back to the others, but he couldn't because of how I was squeezing his neck.

"Chaalee!"

"Chaalee!"

Then I heard the other two running away.

I looked at the cardo on the ground and said, "Sorry, little guy."

By then Yyy and Qqq and Ppp were climbing out of the cylinder.

"What is it, Vvv?" Qqq shouted, pushing past Yyy.

"Food! Get some pipettes. Not you, Yyy. You got yours last night. Now you can stay over there and watch us for a change."

Ppp slid into the cylinder and came back with three pipettes. I held down the cardo while Qqq and Ppp pushed one of the pipettes into the cardo's neck below where my tentacle was and the other two into the thorax.

Yyy sat on a pile of dirt near the tripod and watched the three of us feed. Served him right for being greedy.

It was warm and thick and tasted like metal, like Yyy said. We all took it easy at first because it was so rich, but I could see where it wouldn't take long to get used to this. At least we wouldn't starve. Between the three of us, we drained it pretty quick, but not quick enough to make ourselves sick the way Yyy had. It did give you a headache at first, but I had a feeling that was something that would go away once you got accustomed to the stuff.

I was getting another feeling when I looked at the cloth the cardo had around it. It made me think about what they used to say about the ones with the golden eyes that were supposed to have lived on the Ylla Mountains a long time ago. Myths and legends about how tall they were and how they draped themselves with a shimmering fabric and how they didn't have tentacles because those came along much later, when the race was perfected. I dream about them sometimes, the ones with the golden eyes. You're supposed to report it when you dream about them, but I don't think anyone ever does. I mean, if you report it, then they'd know and then they'd start keeping an eye on you.

Sitting there, sucking the blood through the pipette stuck in its neck, I wondered: Why would a cardo drape itself in cloth?

I thought of an answer, but I didn't like it, so I went back to sucking. Pretty soon the cardo was empty.

We climbed into the cylinder and slept after we ate. Rested, at any rate. Except for Yyy, who shoved himself into his cell face first and made grumbly sorry-for-himself noises that we wouldn't share the cardo with him. Like we didn't all remember what he did with that first one.

This blood made your head buzz. Not in a particularly bad way. It made your brain kind of fizzy and then it made you sleepy. Qqq said we shouldn't try lifting the tripod till we had a chance to digest what we'd had. It was one of those times Qqq actually said something that made sense.

So, we set the portable convector to automatic, sweeping the field. Nothing was going to get close without getting burned.

I fell asleep and the buzz in my head turned into a dream. I was on the Tirra Canal and it was running deep and fast, overflowing in places like it never does anymore. I was in a skimmer, but I wasn't sailing the skimmer. It was sailing itself down the center of the canal and the water hardly made any sound when the bow sliced the surface apart. The water seemed to whisper. Then I started to hear another sound and the sound was the sound of the air moving through those scroll stalks surrounding where we crashed. I looked at the shore and I saw that the scroll stalks were there. On both sides. The sky was the purple it always was, but it had those big blobs of water vapor they have on Earth. They were drifting over the canal. Reflected in the water. And also reflected in the canal were the Ylla Mountains. I looked up, but I couldn't see the mountains ahead of me. It was like they existed in the upside down reflection and nowhere else.

That didn't make any sense, and everything usually makes sense in a dream, even when it doesn't. But the mountains didn't make sense and why the mountains didn't make sense turned into a question. They looked different, the mountains. Not because they were upside down, it was something else. I shouldn't be able to recognize them as the Yllas. But I do. Why? And that woke me up.

•

The big sun was going down when I climbed out of the cylinder. Going down and getting bigger as it got lower. I don't know how that was possible, but that's what it was doing. Something else not to trust about this planet.

The sky was getting darker. The blobs of water vapor were starting to join together. They were getting darker, too. There were still spots where you could see between them, see some of the early stars, but the blobs were closing up, closing off the stars. They looked heavy and they seemed to churn and you could see they'd probably swallow the sun before it went below the horizon.

I went over to where we left the dead cardo and looked at it, shrunken inside the fabric. Maybe the reason their eyes are so small is because of how big the sun is here. That makes sense. I suppose.

I was out there to convince myself there wasn't anything to really worry about; that Ppp couldn't be anything even close to right. But the more I looked down at the dead thing the more I worried. Just because Ppp didn't know what he was talking about didn't make him wrong.

I poked at the body with a nondominant tentacle. There were several layers of fabric under the outer covering, and there was something disturbing about how deliberately the rags were arranged.

The cardo was on its back. I lifted the first layer of fabric covering its thorax. There was a second piece of fabric sewn into the underside of the first and something was held in the pocket created by how the two pieces were fitted together. I reached in with my tentacle and could feel something hard in the pocket. I teased the object out and dropped it on the cardo's thorax. I didn't like the way it felt against my skin.

It was a black folder of an object. Soft. Not fabric, but soft. Like the leather they make from dead cardos. I flicked it open. It was slit across the top, but I didn't see that right away. What I saw first didn't make any sense and that didn't help my mood. There was a square window cut into the folder. Under the window you could see a small image. The light was going so I had to lean close to see any details.

What was behind the little window was an image of a cardo's face. Fabric around its neck and another big piece of fabric behind it, attached to the back of its head like a decoration or headdress or something.

It frightened me, this image.

I leaned back, pushed myself across the dirt until I felt the cylinder touch my tympano. Why would a cardo carry around an image of another cardo? Then I was struck by the really freaky part of all this: Whoever heard of cardos having personal possessions?

I felt very tight all over. I was trying not to shake. Trying not to tremble like Ppp.

Maybe it was a certificate of ownership. Maybe it was like a brand. Something their owners put on them so they could keep track of them. That made sense. For a couple of heartbeats. No, if you were going to brand them, you would brand them. If you were going to track them, you'd attach a tracker. You wouldn't make this loose object and put it in these baggy fabric wraps. It could fall out.

No, it wasn't what I thought it was. I didn't know what it was, but I knew it wasn't what I wanted it to be.

I took a deep breath of that potent air and went back to the dead cardo.

I picked up the folder and pulled it open at the slit to see what was inside. What I found were folded pieces of a different kind of material. It was like the material scrolls are made off. I took one out and unfolded it.

There was a drawing in one corner. A cardo sitting on a kind of throne, all draped in fabric and holding a long stick. And next to the figure there was something I took for a kind of glyphics, combinations of different squiggly symbols set in rows.

I Promise to pay the Bearer on Demand the Sum of One Pound

I didn't know what it meant, but I was growing increasingly certain we hadn't been killing cattle.

I dropped the folder and the certificates and started looking at the outer fabric to see if there were any more pockets. I wish I hadn't done that.

One outside pocket was heavy with something that rattled. I tipped the covered piece of fabric and the contents landed on the dirt next to the dead cardo.

There were pieces of metal, disks of different sizes,

different colors, stamped with figures I couldn't understand. There was one big piece that was more solid than the others with a symmetrical design etched into it. I picked this up and looked at it. It was smooth and it had a little knob at one end and a hinge along part of the opposite side.

Then I realized the object was moving. I could feel it through the tips of my tentacles. A rhythmic vibration. Very light, but unmistakable. And it was making noise. A tiny little tapping, like something knocking from the inside, trying to get out. I thought there was something alive in there. And when I thought that I dropped the object.

It landed in the dirt in front of me and when it landed it opened. The cover popped open on the little hinge and I could see inside.

I leaned down to get a better look.

There wasn't anything alive inside. I wish there had been. Something alive wouldn't have worried me as much as what I saw.

It was a machine. An impossibly small machine. The workings were under a clear quartz-like inner cover, like the clear face of the tripods. There were two flat rods of unequal length joined at the center and pointing to the edge where there were small glyphics cut into a ring.

Under the two rods were these insanely small cogs and gears turning together and in opposition, and something like a spring that coiled and uncoiled, pulsing. Little ratchets and pins moved back and forth, catching and releasing. Tiny regulators and governors, everything synchronized and regimented. Minuscule jewels secured these spinning, gleaming, circularities. The circles were rimmed with little notches. The notches from one circle meshed with the notches on another and held them briefly before letting them slide clear. Then everything moved forward, one carefully incremented step at a time. Everything so small. So golden. So much ornate precision in this tiny shell. I had no idea what it was doing, but I knew it was doing it with an incredible beauty. The tiny spinning disks reminded me of the rings that were supporting the boxes behind the cardos in the field. But these were so small, so polished, so graceful. Tiny pieces of metal dancing in a case that was smaller than the tip of my tentacle.

I looked at the dead one, at the boney pseudos growing out of the knob of flesh at the end of its upper appendage.

Who would give something like this to a cardo?

Then another question blotted out the first: What if the cardos had made it themselves?

The sun was gone now and the boiling darkness had closed up over everything. There was a rumbly growl of a sound coming from the sky, like tremendous empty boilers slamming into each other. Then a stutter of light beyond the dark blur followed by a brighter flash, then another rolling growl.

There was something attached to the inside of the cover that closed over the quartz and the gears. I had to hold it close to my eye to see what it was by the flashes of white light.

It was an image on some flat material cut and pressed into the cover. In the image were two Earth cardos, both draped in fabric, but not the same kind of fabric. One was wearing an arrangement similar to what was wrapped around the dead one across from me. Black shiny covers over its lower pseudos, cloth wrapped around the lower appendages. Several different pieces around the upper torso. Tubular bits around the upper appendages. Something around its neck that didn't look like a restraining device. It had something floppy in its pseudos that looked like a sack that would fit around the articulated ends of the upper limbs. The pseudos.

The other one in the image was encased in something completely different. Where the first was all in black, the second, smaller cardo was all in white. The lower appendages of that one were not separately wrapped, but were contained in a single piece of fabric covering them from the midsection to the ground. The covering on the torso of this one was much more form fitting. It seemed to trace the outline of its body and wrapped the upper appendages with something white, but translucent. And there was a pattern in the translucent covering. The clusters of pseudos were covered with white sacks like the one the dark cardo was holding. In one cluster of pseudos, the white clad cardo was holding a collection of what appeared to be vegetation gathered roughly into a ball. There was more white fabric falling behind the creature, beginning behind the head and cascading to the floor.

They were looking straight out at me from the image. It was a weird feeling looking in those tiny eyes. It all looked strangely ceremonial. Like the record of some kind of ritual.

But cardos have no societal structure. At least not the ones we knew.

I looked at the small image next to all that whirling mechanism. The superior height of the dark one and the evidence of round bulges on the upper torso of the one in white reminded me that cardos came in two varieties. Aside from the different physicality of the two, it's not easy to tell them apart. If you've seen two, you've seen them all.

That's what I was thinking when I realized the cardo in white looked familiar to me. The way the face was arranged. The pinpoint eyes, the thin smudge of a mouth, the fleshy thing where its beak should be.

The next bolt of light and hammer of sound came very close together and synchronized with something coming together in my head. I think I made a noise, but it was lost in the echoes of the sound falling out of the sky. This white cardo was the same white cardo depicted in the image I found in the folder on the dead one.

I went back to the dead cardo. I moved its head so I could see its face. There was a lance of what I later realized were electrical discharges, closer than the others. The features of the creature were blasted with light. Shriveled by Qqq's and Ppp's and my feeding, it was still recognizable as the tall dark cardo in the round image facing the gears.

This time the sound from the clouds began like something cracking open. Something as big as a mountain. The cracking became louder and took on a heavy momentum. Something rolling down from the sky. Rolling my way.

Ceremonially dressed cardos carrying images of each other in tiny little machines.

This is not the behavior of livestock.

We shouldn't be here.

I know I thought it. I might have said it out loud.

Something hit the dirt in front of me with a plop. I scuttled back against the cylinder. We were under attack! Then a couple more plops in the dirt around me. Drops of something. Fat drops of something falling out of the sky. I reached out and one of them hit the end of my tentacle. It was clear and not sticky and didn't smell like anything. I couldn't make the situation any worse so I tasted it. It was water. Coming out of the sky. Those blobs of water vapor were condensing and when the water droplets got heavy enough they fell out of the blobs.

The cardos had figured out a way to keep water vapor in the sky and when they needed it, it would simply fall down on them. How could cardos do that?

More drops. Lots more. Another white flash and the sounds of rolling and crashing. The drops were coming so fast and there were so many of them I couldn't focus on them individually. They came down in a shiny curtain.

I gathered up the golden toy and was going to climb back into the cylinder and show it to Qqq and Yyy and Ppp. But I stopped myself at the lip of the cylinder. What good would it do to tell the others? Ppp would whimper, Qqq would panic, Yyy wouldn't be able to understand what it might mean.

No. If I told them, it wouldn't be of any use to them and, more important, it would render them no use to me. What I needed to do was keep my mouth shut and get on with the job of raising the tripod and moving us away from here. We had to find another cylinder, hopefully one with a full crew and more tripods.

I looked at the golden artifact held in my tentacle. Water drops were hitting the quartz, magnifying the gears and springs and levers. Light and noise from the sky. The jewels in the case flashed red.

I threw the thing away. I coiled my tentacle and threw it as far as I could, out over the field that was still burning, but had started to smoke and hiss under the condensed water vapor.

We shouldn't be here.

The water from the condensed vapor poured into the open cylinder and over me as I climbed down and told the others we had to get a move on. I didn't tell them about what I was thinking. I told them I was afraid the water would collect and create enough mud to keep us from ever getting free. They rousted themselves and we packed all the supplies we could into the cabin and under the cowl of the one operating tripod.

•

Qqq climbed into the command sling behind the motivators, which I knew he would. Yyy took control of the actuators so he could operate the external tentacles. I knew he'd do that. I was happy to hang below the control deck with Ppp and keep an eye on the tripod's power plant. I wasn't down there for long.

Qqq called for power to all systems. The cabin and cowl shook as we engaged the lifters.

Once at our full height, the servos came online and the tripod swayed slightly, standing on its own for the first time.

Then, nothing happened. Nothing continued to happen for a considerable amount of time.

I crawled up from the power plant, Ppp following me. I looked across the control deck. Qqq was swinging gently in the command sling, looking at the controls in front of him as if they were going to bite him.

"Qqq," I said, as firmly yet respectfully as possible. "We should get out of here."

"Yes," he said without looking at me. "That's what I was about to do."

With which Qqq wrapped his tentacles around the two command receptors and moved them forward.

I was pretty certain death was moments away.

The tripod lurched as the foreleg lifted and connected with the ground beyond the pit. Everything tipped backward.

"Auto stabilize!" I called to Qqq.

"What?"

"Engage the auto stabilizer!"

"Right, yes. That's what I was going to do. Where is that, exactly?"

"Down and to the right. The big green lever with 'Auto-stabilizer' stamped on it!"

"Ahhhhh, yes. Right. Yes."

I watched Qqq's eyes dart about the controls until he found the very large, very clearly marked lever for the auto-stabilizer system. He grabbed the lever with his tentacle and pushed it into position. I heard the system engage with the tripod's motors and released the breath I didn't know I was holding.

The lifters adjusted and the horizon reappeared in front of the quartz. The tripod leaned forward, the other two legs stepped out of the pit, and we lurched away from where we'd crashed . . . sorry . . . from our landing site, heading across the countryside.

The direction we traveled in had not been selected by Qqq or any of us. It was the way we were facing when we climbed out of the hole we were in.

This indiscriminate motion was eventually interrupted by Yyy who, for the second time in his life, had a reasonable suggestion.

"We need to find one of those other cylinders, Qqq," he said.

"Yes," Qqq said. "Give me some coordinates. We'll need some coordinates."

"Aren't we supposed to have a map?" Ppp asked.

"What good's a map if you don't know where you are?" Yyy said.

I knew what we were supposed to do. I'd heard the same spools Qqq had, but if I shouted instructions at Qqq he'd never listen to me.

"Excuse me, Qqq?" I said, lifting the tip of my tentacle. "I think I remember you saying something about all the cylinders and tripods having locator beacons we could use to find each other."

I could see the side of Qqq's head as he looked through the cowling shield, streaked with condensed water vapor. His mouth was slightly open as he tried to remember a conversation we never had. Meanwhile we galumphed into the darkness ahead.

Then Qqq figured out a way to find out what he assumed he'd forgotten.

"Yeah," he started. "I remember you and me talking about that, Vvv. Remind me how that works again."

"Well, Qqq," I said. "The way you explained it to me was that when a cylinder lands it transmits a beacon so other crews can find it and we can combine forces."

"Right," Qqq said. "We should do that. They might need our help when they land."

We kept marching through the night, Qqq with his tentacles hovering vaguely over the controls.

"Say, Yyy, didn't you mention the communication tools were by the external tentacle actuators?"

"Ahhhh, yeah, I think so," Yyy was smart enough to play along. "I think I remember that's where Qqq said they were."

"Actuators." Qqq had started to repeat random words he picked out of the conversation going on around him.

"That's right, Qqq," I said. "You might want one of us to take a look, maybe turn on that beacon localizer you mentioned."

"Beacon localizer?"

This was taking forever. Any moment Qqq was going to parade us over a cliff.

"Yyy, how about you go over there and do what Qqq's telling you to do and turn on the beacon localizer?"

"Gosh, Vvv, that sounds like a great idea. I'm sure glad Qqq came up with it."

"You want to know another good idea I remember Qqq telling me about?" I said as Yyy scrambled over to the communication tools.

"Hey, if it was anything near as good as Qqq's other ideas, I'd sure like to hear it, Vvv."

"He said you could link the beacon localizer to the auto-stabilizer and the tripod could walk itself right to the closest cylinder without any input from Qqq. Matter of fact, he could keep his tentacles off the controls and let the machine do its job."

"Controls?"

"That's another great idea, Qqq. Maybe we should do that. I think I know how. Remember, Qqq, you showed me."

I nudged Yyy toward the communication tools.

"Yeah, and I think you should do that right away, Yyy, before something bad happens. We wouldn't want anything bad to happen and spoil this really great start we have. Remember what Qqq always says: 'Enthusiasm Makes The Difference.'"

"He's sure right about that, Vvv."

"Enthusiasm." Qqq whispered, his tentacles hanging down at his sides, twitching slightly.

Yyy didn't have any trouble turning on the localizer and linking it to the auto-stabilizer. All he had to do was follow the instructions on the screen and tap the right options with the tip of his dominant tentacle. The tripod came to a nice smooth stop and we could hear the helio dish being lifted through the hatch in the cowling then humming as it turned and scanned for signals. It went around once, then twice, then it stopped with a good solid thunk. A moment later there were glowing glyphics scrolling up from the bottom of Yyy's screen.

"Vvv! It worked! It found another cylinder! We're not alone!" Yyy was almost squealing, like a new bud fresh after separation.

The glyphics offered him options, asking him what he wanted the tripod to do. He tapped the screen and told it we wanted to find the others.

There was a rumble underneath the cabin and the turret rotated about ninety degrees. Then the tripod started to walk, carefully, confidently, in the direction we were facing.

The glyphics told us we'd reach the other cylinder before the next sunset.

It kept on raining. And there were electrical discharges all over the sky. I came to associate the electrical discharges with the booming sounds.

•

"Maybe we should just kill him," Yyy said.

We'd left Ppp with Qqq, who was still sitting in the command sling. We told Ppp to make sure Qqq didn't touch anything.

Yyy and I were under the turret, where we knew what was said would be lost in the noise of the tripod hiking toward our "comrades," as Qqq kept calling them.

"Why do you want to kill him?" I asked.

"I don't think he's up to the burdens of command."

"Well, that's because he isn't a commander. Frankly, I think he's the one who killed the commander."

"You think Qqq killed Ddd?"

"Like the thought never occurred to you?"

"It does sort of make sense, doesn't it?"

"Why do you want to kill him now?"

"Like I said, I don't think he's up to it."

"What does he have to be up to? The glyphics tell us what to do."

"But when we get there and they ask him about what happened with the cardos and the convector, how we killed them, and he's supposed to tell them we got attacked and how we're heroes. I don't think he can carry that off. Do you?"

71

"For all we know what happened to us happened to the other crews. I agree with you, Qqq is useless, but I don't want to have to explain killing him if I don't have to."

"I thought we ought to be sure. Get our stories straight."

"You know what? I'm less worried about getting in trouble than I am about getting killed."

"They're a bunch of cardos!"

I could have told him what I was beginning to think about the Earth creatures. Maybe I should have. Maybe he had a right to know. Anyway, before I could let him in on what I'd found out, the decision was taken away from me.

For a moment I thought it was more noise from the electrical discharges, but as soon as I thought that I knew it was different. This wasn't a rumble, it was an explosion. Not close, but not far away.

I looked at Yyy, Yyy looked at me, but before either of us could say anything there was this sound that got louder and closer. The whole tripod oscillated as something shrieked over our heads. Then there was the slam of a pressure wave along with another explosion.

We were starting to climb out of the turret and into the cabin when the tripod lurched again, this time not because of something external, but because of something the machine was doing. The machine was running.

I was thrown back against the main turret ring and saw my dominant tentacle come that close to being snatched up by the thrust bearing. By the time I scrambled away from the bearing I could see Yyy heading up the ladder to the control deck. I followed him, but he stopped in the hatchway. I had to squeeze past him, which was really much closer than I ever wanted to be to Yyy.

When I got past Yyy, I saw what had stopped him.

We were looking at the command sling where poor Ppp was struggling with Qqq who had grabbed the controls. That action automatically disengaged the auto-stabilizer. Now Qqq was driving the tripod forward, pushing the attitude of the machine, and its speed, into the red zone.

"Stop him!" I yelled at Ppp.

"That's what I'm trying to do," he called back as he struggled to get his tentacles around Qqq and pull him away from the controls.

There was another screaming approach of something. It shot past the side of the tripod, closer than the first projectile. Whatever it was hit the dirt ahead of us.

A great bubble of ground blossomed in front of the tripod, thrown up by chunks of orange and white flame.

Ppp looked back at Yyy and me.

"I think someone's shooting at us."

Both Yyy and myself were in agreement with Ppp's conclusion.

Yyy and I squeezed past Ppp and got our tentacles around Qqq then worked to dislodge him from the controls. It wasn't easy. Each time we pulled on Qqq's tentacles gripping the controls the tripod responded violently, magnifying the struggle.

"Run!" Qqq was shouting. "Run away and establish a new perimeter!"

As soon as we got one of Qqq's tentacles off a control he'd flail it around and start hitting us. If we let go of him to try to grab the tentacle, he'd grab hold of the controls again and send us lurching and stumbling across the dark terrain.

Something else shot past the cabin and hit the ground off

to one side, closer than the earlier projectiles.

In light of the situation, Yyy took this moment to actually think about what was happening and drew a conclusion he stated as a question.

"That's not the cardos shooting at us, is it? How could it be the cardos?"

Qqq was flailing away at me with his tentacles, raising welts on the top of my head, so I felt it wasn't the best time to bring Yyy up to speed with what I was thinking.

"Get him off me. Get him away from the controls," I shouted.

That's when Ppp came around in front of the three of us and hit Qqq between the eyes with a gas canister. This stunned Qqq, but it still took three more blows before he let go of the controls and slumped back against Yyy and me.

With no manual input from the controls, the tripod leveled itself and came to a stable stop as we dragged Qqq to the back of the cabin. He was groggy, but not completely unconscious.

"Enthusiasm, enthusiasm is what we lack," he mumbled.

"Hit him again," I said to Ppp, who obliged. Qqq slumped to the deck, his eyes flickered, then closed.

Yyy nudged me with his dominant tentacle. "I told you we should have killed him."

"Never mind him. We have to move."

"But we're stable," Yyy whined.

Another shell hit the ground behind us.

"Listen," I said squeezing Yyy's head between my tentacles the same way he had squeezed me back before we crashed which felt like a million years ago. "They're shooting at us and if we stay in one place they'll get the range and we'll all be dead."

"Are you trying to tell me the cardos are doing this?"

I left Yyy squatting there with an impenetrably stupid look on his face and went to climb up to the controls. There was no way I could do a worse job of guiding the tripod than Qqq had.

The motion inputs were all on one control stick. Everything else, moving the turret, firing the convectors, were on the other control stick. There were pedals on the floor that charged the convectors and raised and lowered the whole machine.

I grabbed the controls with the intent of going in the opposite direction from where the projectiles were coming, but as I was doing that there was a screech and something glanced off the side of the cabin. We all looked through the forward port as another projectile tumbled away and hit the ground, having skimmed off the tripod. A degree or two more and it would have decapitated our machine.

I don't know why, I'd never been susceptible to this kind of rage before, but the desire to escape vanished and I spun the turret back toward the source of the shells and pushed the tripod forward.

There wasn't much more than darkness ahead of us. But in the darkness were sharp white sparks and then an orange blister of fire I thought had to be the source of the large projectiles they were throwing at us. I started walking the tripod toward the sparks and fire.

"What are you doing?" I could hear Yyy shouting up at me. "We're supposed to be running away, not running toward!"

"Shut up!" I shouted back and, to my surprise, that's what he did.

What I learned in that moment when the shell creased the side of the tripod was this: When someone is shooting at you, things become very clear. Anger wins over everything. Even fear.

I did not like the idea of someone trying to kill me, even if they were nothing but cardos. I forgot all about wanting to understand the intelligence behind those sparks of light and those plumes of fire. All of a sudden I wanted to do what we came here to do: Invade the hell out of this crummy planet.

More sparks and more tongues of fire, but we were moving too fast for them to get the range and the shells went singing past us. If they got a lucky shot we'd be finished, but I have to tell you, in that instant, I didn't care one way or the other.

"Prime the main convector!" I shouted.

"Yes, sir!"

It was Ppp who responded. I looked back and saw him pushing open the plates and pumping the shank to energize the non-conductivity chambers. Yyy was over by Qqq, a canister in his tentacles should our leader regain consciousness.

"Yyy, stand by the actuators."

And Yyy didn't challenge me. He put down the canister and moved to the exterior tentacle actuators.

In the time I spent looking back at the others, we'd covered a lot of ground. We were much closer to the enemy now and I could make out some details. Clusters of cardos working the whatever it was that was throwing the projectiles. Long tubes. Cannons! Not launching tubes, but cannons. There were other cardos holding bundles in their upper appendages. The bundles generated the sequence of sparks.

There were boxes set on platforms supported by round braces and more of the long-faced thoat sort of creatures. Work animals. Work animals the cardos controlled?

"Convectors charged and ready!" Ppp called up to me.

I saw another sequence of white sparks, this time followed by the hard sounds of small objects hitting the side of the tripod. They sounded like angry pebbles. I decided whatever was making the sparks was hurling tiny projectiles at us.

Two more orange flames. Two more projectiles going wide and above us. They weren't aiming anymore, they were firing wild. They were too scared to aim. Good.

More sparks, more pebbles. But we were closer now and the pebbles had more energy. A string of punctures marched across the skin of the cabin. Hot little knobs of something bounced around inside the cowl until they were spent.

Time to end this.

I took control of the central front mounted convector and discharged it while making a wide sweeping motion with the oculus across the line of cardos and their weapons.

It was like painting a line of fire across them. The sparks stopped. Little stick figures of flame ran and fell. Where the convector ray hit the sources of the orange puffs the effect was more dramatic. There must have been stores of whatever explosives they were using to launch the shells. The explosives were sensitive to heat and when the convector beam touched them there was a deep thud that shook the cabin. The weapon sites were swallowed by smoke and undulating fire. Flaming pieces of metal and cardo went spinning through the night, trailing curls of smoke lit from below.

And then it was quiet except for the rain hitting the cowling. I lifted my tentacles from the controls and the tripod came to a gentle halt in front of all that fire.

And for a moment, I understood the appeal of enthusiasm.

•

The cardos had solved one problem. Qqq was dead.

I was still at the controls when Yyy came up behind me.
"You better have a look at Qqq."
Qqq was slumped against the bulkhead, a row of tiny holes stretching across his face and through one eye. The last stutter of pellets that breached the hull had drilled a neat dotted line into his head.
"Well, you wanted us to get our story straight. It can't be much straighter than this," I said as I closed Qqq's other eye.
"What do you mean, Vvv?"
"Qqq died a hero, you idiot," I said. "He led us into battle and blew up the enemy and died at the controls of the tripod."
I looked at Yyy. I watched the concept slowly upload to his brain. It took a long time before he started to smile and finally said, "Oh, I get it."
I stood there wishing in a funny way it had been Yyy who'd gotten himself killed. There'd be no need for a story if Yyy was dead because nobody would care.
"Why don't you turn the auto-stabilizer back on and get us going to the other cylinder?"
"Good idea."
"Thanks."

Yyy went to relink the communications tools to the auto-stabilizer. I turned around and there was Ppp, looking past me to Qqq's body. Ppp actually looked sad.

"Help me cover him up, Ppp."

"Sure."

We got a vacuum bag from a locker and put Qqq into it. The tripod started back on its way to the other cylinder while Ppp and I were mopping up what little blood there was on the deck. I realized Ppp was looking at me more than he was mopping.

"What is it?" I asked him.

"The cardos. They're not really cardos, are they? I mean, like the cardos we have."

"Whatever they look like, they are not cardos."

"Could they be the highest intelligence on this planet?"

"You better hope so."

"Why?"

"Because if they aren't the highest intelligence, if this place has got something even smarter . . . "

I was too frightened by the possibilities of what I was saying to finish the sentence.

Ppp knew what I was talking about. He looked at me, trying to think of something to say. Eventually he said, "Maybe you should rest or something."

"Rest?"

"I'll keep an eye on Yyy, make sure he doesn't touch the controls."

"Yeah, maybe I should rest."

"Go ahead."

I left Ppp to finish vacuum-packing Qqq's body, went around the bulkhead to where the hammocks were slung and climbed into the closest one. I thought I'd rest for a little while. I think I rocked back and forth twice, maybe three times, and then I was dreaming. Back on the Tirra Canal.

The rocking of the hammock became the rocking of the skimmer. When I opened my eyes, I mean opened my eyes in the dream, that's where I was. The Tirra Canal, still running fast and deep and overflowing in places. I looked down and there were the Ylla Mountains reflected in the surface like before. But this time, when I looked up I saw the mountains themselves, sitting on the horizon with the purple sky behind them. I knew they were the Ylla Mountains, but they didn't look like they do now. Now they're old mountains, smoothed and rounded by wind and water and time. But in my dream they were young mountains, freshly stabbed up into the sky like blades of stone and crystal. They were the Yllas the way they looked a long time ago.

The skimmer took me closer to the mountains. I could see flashes and trails of light coming off great slanting crystals growing out of the living rock.

It was important for me to keep going, to get closer to the mountains so I could figure out what those flashes meant. I stared at them, trying to see detail beyond the sharp light reflected from the crystals, but the harder I looked the less I could see and the more my eyes hurt until I had to look away, look down at the water splitting under the bow.

I shut my eyes in the dream and I listened to the water slipping under the bow, sliding around the skimmer, and somehow that made my eyes hurt less. Then I heard something in the sliding sound of the water. It was a voice, not speaking, but singing.

A very smooth, pleasant voice. Soft, higher than voices

usually are. I didn't know the song the singer was singing. Then I heard one word I knew: "Ulla." Not shouted like we shout it, but sung. Very softly.

I wanted to see who the singer was, so I opened my eyes. But when I opened my eyes I was back in the cabin and it was full of orange light coming in hard and straight through the quartz face of the tripod's cabin. And I could see that suspiciously big sun climbing over a hill ahead of us. It stopped raining while I was asleep.

Then I realized we weren't moving.

I pulled myself out of the hammock and went around the bulkhead. The big brute of a sun blinded me. How can Earth creatures stand it being so big and so close?

I squinted as the shape of Ppp rose up in front of me and blocked the sun. He looked worried.

"Yyy stopped the tripod," he said.

It must have been the tripod stopping that pulled me out of my dream.

"Why?"

"He told me to mind my own business."

I went around Ppp and headed for the controls. Yyy was in the command sling, looking out at the sunrise, his tentacles off the controls.

The ground underneath us was moving. Or it looked like it was moving. I leaned against the quartz and watched a herd of animals surrounding the treads of the tripod. They were about the size of calots but they were covered with a pale, soft-looking material. Like a misguided attempt at camouflage that made them resemble the blobs of water vapor drifting overhead.

"What made the tripod stop, Yyy?"

He shifted his bulk and looked back at me.

"Vvv, listen, I've been thinking."

I was immediately skeptical of how this conversation was going to go.

"Thinking about what, Yyy?"

"Maybe we shouldn't rush into this."

"Rush into what?

"Ddd is dead, Qqq is dead, the others are dead, it's the three of us with nobody in charge, right?"

I didn't say anything. Yyy took that as a good sign and continued.

"Maybe what we should do before we go looking for the other cylinder is consider all the options."

"Can I get you to point out some of those options for me, Yyy, so I know what you're talking about?"

"I don't see much point in looking for trouble, is all I'm saying. We've got an obligation to look out for ourselves under the circumstances. Why should we be in such a big hurry to join up with another cylinder?"

"For starters, they know we're coming. They knew that when we connected to the beacon. It works both ways."

"That's one of the options I was thinking about. We could turn the beacon off. If anybody ever asks, we say something went wrong with it and we got lost, and by the time we fixed it, the ones in the other cylinder had stopped waiting for us."

"So, instead of linking up with the others you want us to wander around the countryside for a couple of days and wait and see if this whole thing blows over?"

"That's sort of the general direction of my thinking, yes."

"What happened to all that enthusiasm, Yyy?"

"Hey, I'm still loaded with enthusiasm. Nobody's got more enthusiasm than me. But I'm thinking, you know, operationally speaking, the situation has changed and we should reassess our mission."

"The only thing that's changed about the mission is that those little grubs are shooting at us."

"Yeah, well, there's that, too."

"Yyy, it's an invasion. Invasions usually involve a certain amount of violence."

"Sure, but I didn't figure on there being so much violence coming from the other side, that's all."

This from the one who gave me a hard time about my attitude when we were a million miles in space. The ones like Yyy, when it comes to wars, they're in it for the stories they'll tell later. That's why it's so important to them that they don't get killed. I looked at Ppp.

"What do you say, Ppp? Should we do what we came here to do, or do you want to dig a big hole and crawl into it?"

Yyy nudged me with a tentacle. I slapped it away.

"Don't ask him," Yyy said.

"Why not? He should get a vote."

"He's just going to say whatever you want him to say. He likes you."

Yyy said this and instantly knew what a big mistake he'd made. You could see it on his face. He looked like he wanted to snatch the words back with his tentacles and eat them. But the damage was done. He had insulted Ppp. Ppp had some pride left. We all have some pride. Even the ones who aren't entitled to any.

"I don't need anybody telling me how to vote," Ppp said, pulling himself forward. "I vote we find the others and start fighting instead of running away."

I looked at Yyy. All that thinking and look where it got him. He climbed down from the command sling and sulked off behind the bulkhead. I looked at the controls. We had to get moving. Regardless of what any one of us wanted, we couldn't stand there in a field surrounded by fluffy animals. You have to keep moving or you're dead.

So I climbed into the command sling, mainly to keep Yyy from sneaking back in front of the controls, and told Ppp to turn the auto-stabilizer back on, relink it to the beacons, and put us back on the beam to the other cylinder. Ppp jumped to the task. I was starting to worry Ppp was burning off some of that very valuable fear and terror, replacing it with something less stable: Enthusiasm.

We started marching again.

•

If I'd let Yyy decide for us I figured our chances for survival would be slim at best. Not that they were so much better with me in charge. I did not want to be in charge. The last thing I ever wanted in my life was to be in charge of anything.

Maybe Ppp did want to fight, maybe he didn't. Maybe I manipulated him to get what I wanted. I wanted to find the other cylinder, the other Martians, so I wouldn't have to make any more decisions. I wanted to find a group I could stand at the back of and not be noticed. I know I got a little crazy when the fighting started, but you can't count on a feeling like that to last. Under that ugly, swollen sun, my enthusiasm wasn't directed toward anything more sophisticated than survival.

We followed the beam, tramping across the countryside as fast I felt was safe. The ground was mostly mild hills and fields regimented for agriculture.

Maybe the Earth creatures don't eat each other. I hadn't thought about that much, but I suppose it was possible. On Mars we kept our cardos alive by feeding them processed red creeper. Those fluffy creatures like calots and the thoats, maybe they eat them.

There were gray and sandy-colored ribbons climbing around the hills and running in straight lines across the flat parts. I thought they were roads or paths. There wasn't anything on them. Which made me start to wonder how many Earth creatures there were on the planet. That got me thinking maybe we could pull this off. I mean, if there weren't that many of them.

Then I saw something else on the flat parts and I stopped thinking about how we might be able to get this to work. What I saw were like the roads, but straighter and darker, and there were two threads of metal running parallel along each path. And they went on for miles, straight as a shot. The kind of straight you get when someone's done a lot of work to make sure they'll be straight.

You could lose yourself staring at them, following them, watching the reflection of the sun running ahead on the metal strips. I guess that's what happened to me. I started to become lost in the points of light bouncing off the metal. Always ahead of you, leading you on, pulling you toward something. Shiny like the shards of crystal I saw in the mountains in my dream.

"Do you hear that?"

Ppp was next to me. I hadn't noticed him coming up to the controls.

"Hear what?"

"Listen," he said, lifting one tentacle, pointing up and holding it there, like an antenna, to catch what he was hearing.

Nothing for a moment. Or nothing I could separate from the sounds the tripod made as it walked. Then I heard it, too.

A note. A long high note. Almost like the mechanical calls tripods make between them when they work the ice caps.

"What is that?" Ppp said. He was trying to decide if it was something to be afraid of.

"I don't know."

And then we saw it. It came from behind us along the metal and streaked past us, belching smoke from a cone toward the front end.

The thing on the gleaming threads was black and metal and tube shaped at the front with a square box at the back. And it had those circles, like the round supports on the boxes where we crashed. The circles were turning, turning very quickly, along the threads. It was following the threads. Not following, wedged between them. The multiple circles spun, and that moved the metal beast forward. Moving so fast. Ppp and I stared at it as it passed under us and charged away along the strips.

Behind the tube there were other boxes, linked together, with rows of square holes punched in the sides. Ppp and I could see little pink faces at the holes. Earth cardos leaning out and looking up at us.

The machine was transporting them. That's how they got around.

The piercing noise came with a blast of white vapor that shot up into the air over the lead box, mixing with the black cloud coming from a cone at the front. The smoke opened up and spread and lifted up into the air. Maybe it never came down. What was the point of that? There were orange sparks mixed with the black smoke.

The circles turned faster than ever, blurring, becoming a spinning arrangement of disks pulling the whole assemblage forward.

"Should we stop it?" Ppp whispered to me.

It occurred to me we should do something, so I pushed the chargers to get the main convector ready and moved the control so the oculus was pointing at the sequence of metal boxes roaring away from us. I tapped the sights a little so I was leading the machine, ready to send the convector energy down the length of the oculus.

But I didn't. I don't know why. Wasn't that the whole point of our being here? Maybe, but I didn't trigger the convector.

I took my tentacles from the weapon controls and leaned back. Ppp saw what I was doing, but he didn't say anything.

It was getting away, moving faster, leaving us behind as we lumbered at a steady pace alongside the dark path and the threads of metal. We could have destroyed that machine. Destroyed it and everything on it. But we didn't. I don't know why, but we didn't. Why I didn't.

Maybe we could pull this off, the invasion. Maybe. But

it seemed to be getting more complicated with each step we took. And complications are never good.

Ppp and I watched the machine. Watched it get farther ahead of us and disappear around a hill. We could still follow the trail of smoke it left in the sky. The smoke stretched out behind it and thinned, like it was coming apart as it rose. It wasn't like Martian black smoke. That smoke is dense and heavy and falls to the ground and starts killing right away.

•

I didn't think it was possible to feel as happy as I did when we came over that last hill and saw the ground had been scorched by an incoming cylinder. I followed the path of burned vegetation and there was the cylinder, surrounded by a smaller gulley than the one where we crashed. They must have had a much smoother time of it.

There were two tripods at the edge of this camp, one completely raised, the other low on its risers while a half dozen Martians transferred supplies from the cylinder to the hold. So many Martians! And alive!

They saw us coming, and the air was filled with exultations.

"Alloo! Alloo! Ulla!"

We answered in kind. Ppp and I were at the controls. Yyy climbed up when he heard the noise. He looked forward, at the two tripods and all he could muster was a wet snort and "I hope they've got something to eat."

They did have something for us to eat. There were three

cardos lashed to the side of the cylinder waiting for us.

The one in charge of the group was Hhh and he was the original commander of his cylinder. They had lost five Martians between the launch and the heat when they punched through all that rich air. One of the three tripods was damaged in the crash.

We told Hhh what happened to us. Most of what happened to us. And the story made sense to him. He said there had been problems with some of the other cylinders. Hhh essentially commandeered our tripod and folded us into his unit bringing it back to three operating tripods. I had no objections. We weren't on our own any more.

I asked Hhh what he meant about there being problems. He said he'd talk to me about it after we'd had something to eat.

They took Qqq's body out of the tripod for us. We crossed his face with distillate, burned him, read from the scrolls, then scattered the ashes.

I had some cardo, but I didn't have much of an appetite. I kept thinking of that metal rolling machine Ppp and I saw on our travels. I kept seeing those spinning circular objects on the sides and how they were like big, heavy versions of the small, complex gold gears and pivots in the case I found on the Earth cardo. Cattle don't make machines, but the cardos did. At least the cardos here did. Different kinds of machines. Big brutes that charge across the landscape, miniature universes packed into golden cases, and devices to fire stuttering pebbles that punch a string of lethal holes in your face.

I left Ppp and Yyy to eat their fill and went looking for Hhh.

He was up in our tripod, examining the damage.

"You've had a rough time, haven't you, Vvv?"

"I guess so. But we're here now."

"Yes, here we are indeed," he said and turned to look out the quartz face of the cabin. He stood there, looking out at the hills and the sky and the blobs of water vapor, not talking. I finally worked up the nerve to say something.

"You mentioned some of the other cylinders had trouble," I said.

I wasn't sure if he was listening, then he sighed and turned to me. He looked at me for a long time, like he was trying to size me up. What happens after someone does that to you is almost never anything good.

"The invasion has not gone as smoothly as planned, Vvv."

"How much not smoothly, if I'm allowed to ask?"

"There were assumptions and miscalculations, Vvv," he said. I tried to look like I was surprised by this information.

Hhh went on to tell me what he'd heard and experienced. I think he was glad to have someone he could talk to about what was going on, it didn't have to be me. Could have been anybody. My luck, it was me.

Some of the cylinders never made it off the surface, Hhh told me. They blew up in the launching tubes and scooped out huge craters on the plateau. A couple fell back and crashed. Adjustments were made and the launches continued.

Of the cylinders that made it to Earth, close to half were lost when they fell into what was erroneously thought to be the massive blue lava flows that covered much of the surface. Turned out it wasn't lava, it was water. Oceans of the stuff. The landing strategists lacked sufficient imagination to conceive of a planet with so much water. Leadership had the landing strategists removed. Summarily, expeditiously, publicly.

Some cylinders hammered into the ground cap first, trapping the crews inside. One of the objectives Hhh was tasked with was to locate these head first cylinders and try to rescue the crews or at least salvage the equipment.

Hhh knew of no cylinder that made it to Earth with its crew intact. Some died at launch, some died on the way, some burned or were crushed when they landed.

And then there were the cylinders that missed the Earth completely. My fear when we were tumbling through space turned out to be very real for some Martians. They skidded off the edge of the atmosphere and were now on their way out of the solar system, beyond hope of rescue. That gave me a real chill. The idea of those crews out there forever. Maybe someday someone will find the derelicts and look inside. What will they make of us then?

Hhh continued that the mood at home remained relatively positive. But there had been protests. Certain groups had started to question the whole idea of the invasion, declaring it a waste of precious time and resources. Members of these groups were dealt with by the same judiciary workers who took care of the failed landing strategists. They did so using similar methods.

"Not smooth, Vvv," Hhh summed it up. "Not anything you would call smooth."

Hhh looked at me and he must have seen what I was thinking. He put his dominant tentacle around my head.

"But I believe we can still do the job we were sent to

do. The capabilities of these cardos caught us off guard, no good saying they didn't. But we're ready for them now. And reinforcements are on the way. If we stay the course we'll be in good shape by the time they get here."

"What exactly is the course, Hhh?"

"Suppress the indigenous population and eliminate their ability to retaliate. Simple."

"Simple."

"As soon as all three tripods are stocked and checked out, we're to head south, assess the capabilities of the cardos along the way, and eliminate any resistance. We can still do this, Vvv. We'll be okay."

I wasn't sure if he was talking to me or to himself. But I was glad he didn't mention enthusiasm.

We stayed in the cabin, looking out at the camp and the others. I finally worked up the nerve to ask him what I couldn't stop thinking about.

"Hhh, has anybody run into anything in charge of the cardos?"

He knew what I was asking.

"No. All sorts of animals, many of them warm blooded. This planet is choking with life. But no evidence of any intelligence above the cardos. They appear to be the dominant species on this planet."

"But they're cardos." I was still having trouble understanding how this was possible.

"Certainly not like the ones we found on Venus, or the wild ones they used to catch up in the Ylla Mountains."

"But they are the same animal, aren't they?"

"It would appear so, but they'll need to be examined and studied to confirm that."

"How does the same animal show up on different planets? And why are the ones here so much more . . . "

"Dangerous?"

"I was going to say developed."

Hhh moved away from me, past the edge of the quartz. He was in shadow when he turned back to look at me. All I could see was the sheen of his eyes.

"Nobody planned for anything like this," he said from the darkness. "The Earth creatures are more intelligent than we could have imagined, and we're paying for that arrogance. But they're as mortal as we are."

"How did they get here?" I asked.

"Maybe they started here."

"How could they have started here and on Mars and on Venus…"

"And who knows where else?"

"Where else?"

"If they're on three planets, in slightly different variations, why can't they be on three hundred planets, or three thousand? Maybe there's something so basic about their primitive life form that they spontaneously spring up all over the universe."

"Why?"

"When you start asking that question, Vvv, you nudge dangerously close to religion. And that's not going to help us on the battlefield."

Hhh stepped out of the shadows. I wondered how old he was. He came to my side and we looked out at the Martians who had come so far with us.

"We have plans and contingencies," he said, sounding

very tired and not altogether confident of what he was saying. "We'll adapt. If we move quickly, if they don't have any more surprises for us, we can break them. There'll be time enough to figure out what they are or where they came from once we put them down and keep them down. But the situation is in flux at the moment. I think you understand that, Vvv."

"We brought the invasion," I said. "But they started the war."

"And nobody ever wins a war, Vvv. Wars always come down to making the other side lose faster than yours."

We stayed in the cabin a while. Talking. Mostly about Mars.

•

Ppp and Yyy joined me under the cowl after they'd eaten and rested and I told them about Hhh's plan. We would form a triangle with Hhh's tripod at the point, keeping each other in sight, and move in an equatorial direction, doing what destruction we thought appropriate along the way, but expressly on Hhh's order. That was my favorite part of the plan: Not doing anything until somebody told me what to do.

Ppp liked the specificity of the instructions. I think they made him feel like a real soldier. Yyy grumbled.

In the morning, the triangle of tripods started moving across the fields and hills and if you saw us like that you'd actually think we knew what we were doing.

The sky was crowded with a burbling canopy of dark

gray water vapor. After a while it started to condense and fall on us as we went on our way. It didn't fall hard, like the other night. This was soft, gentle. Streaking down the quartz as we went.

There were more paths and more straight runs of metal, but no more hulking machines. Sometimes there were small knots of cardos on the paths. When they saw us they ran, some along the paths, some breaking away and stumbling across the hills or the flat parts, whatever the terrain was at that particular moment. We ate before we left so there was no particular reason to bother with the ones we saw along the way.

Ppp was looking at the threads of metal going by.

"Maybe that's their idea of a tripod," he said.

"What's their idea of a tripod?"

"That engine thing we saw that ran on the metal . . . what would you call them? Pipes? Rails? Maybe that's how they get around."

"You could only go where the pipes go."

"Maybe they'll figure out a way to do it without the pipes some day."

"Not if we have anything to say about it."

Ppp looked a little disappointed at this.

"Listen, Ppp, I'm sorry, but you better get it straight what we're doing here. We're here to keep Mars alive, and that's all. We're not here to help the cardos. We're not supposed to raise their standard of living. I admit, the cardos here seem to be smarter than the ones we have at home. But that's evolution. Evolution is how we got to be who we are today. It's why we do the invading instead of being invaded by somebody else, because of how fast we evolved, how we got so much better as a species."

"Do you believe the stories about the old ones with the golden eyes?"

"That's not science, Ppp, that's mythology. You shouldn't talk about that kind of nonsense."

"Did you ever get up there? In the Ylla Mountains before they closed them down?"

"Once, when I was a bud."

"What was it like?"

I turned around, to see if Yyy was anywhere around. He was below. I didn't want him hearing any of this.

"Look," I started. "It was different back then. It was before the rectification, before everything was all straightened out. Nobody ever lived up there. It was a legend. A myth. And it took up space in your head that was needed for more important matters."

"But you did see the mountains once?"

"I saw them, they were mountains."

"Were there crystals?"

"I think so."

"Crystals right on the mountains?"

"More like in the mountains, part of the mountains. They never stopped the skimmer, they never let us get a good look. They said it was dangerous. They used to let you poke around for bits of tile, chunks of crystal, but they stopped that. They said there were dangerous mineral deposits, so you couldn't stay there long or you'd get sick."

"So you never saw any of the old ones?"

"There was nobody there. And there never were any old ones. It's a story somebody made up."

"I think I saw one."

"Saw one what?"

"An old one."

I leaned over and put my dominant tentacle around Ppp's head and pulled him close to my face.

"If Yyy ever hears you talk like that, he'll toss you to the public health wardens before you could spit in his eye."

"Not for real," Ppp stuttered. I'd scared him. "But once when I was asleep. I saw something and I knew it was an old one. I don't know how I knew, I just knew. That's how dreams work, I guess."

I should have slapped him and told him to shut up. I should have told him to go lubricate the turret bearings and clean the convector chambers. But I didn't. Instead I asked him a question.

"What do you think you saw in your dream?"

Ppp looked down through the quartz and was quiet so long I thought he'd decided to end the conversation. Then he started talking without looking at me, focusing on those silver pipes going by under the tripod.

"In the dream, I'm on the Plains of Barso," Ppp began. "The part that feels like it goes on forever. I'm standing in front of this big thing I've never seen before, but I know it's some kind of ship. It doesn't look like any kind of ship I've ever seen. It's long and slender and gleaming silver. It tapers to a point at one end, then the point keeps going, getting thinner and thinner, like a needle. The opposite end tapers too, but not as much. That end has a kind of mouth or exhaust. And there are these blades, these swept-back fins along the back and at the side toward the blunt end. There's a ramp going up the side to a hinged port that opens to the inside of the ship. That's where the old ones are. Dark-skinned and golden-eyed. Walking, almost drifting up the ramp and going inside this ship. They have fabric draped over their shoulders, hanging down to the ground. Not rags like the cardos we saw when we landed, but shimmering white. They're tall and smooth and beautiful, the way the silver ship is beautiful.

"I looked around and I couldn't see any Martians like me, and when I turned back to the ship, the last couple of old ones were drifting up the ramp and going inside.

"That's when the last of the old ones comes over and looks down at me and smiles and says, 'Don't think of this as goodbye.'

"'But you're leaving, right?' I said to him. Except I know he's not a him. He's something else. He . . . whatever it was . . . had a different voice from the rest of us. Smooth and silvery, like the ship. Gentle.

"'Yes, but don't think of this as a goodbye,' whatever it is says to me.

"'Then what is it?' I ask.

"And this he-who-isn't-a-he keeps smiling and then he, it, reaches out and puts the end of their arm, where it breaks up into pseudos, like on a cardo, but slimmer and really delicate and beautiful, puts it on the top of my head and looks at me with those beautiful golden eyes.

"'Take care of yourself,' it says to me. Then it turns around and goes up the ramp to the ship, and the ramp folds into the ship and the hatch closes.

"Then there's the sound of something opening along the spine of the ship and these soft round shapes start coming up out of the back of the ship and getting larger, filling with something. They're bags and they're filling with gas. I don't know how I know this, but I do because it's a dream.

"There are three of these bags, silver and tethered to the

ship by a net. And when they're filled all the way they're bigger than the ship itself. These three round bags moving in the breeze, bumping into each other, making hollow thumping noises like a big drum underwater.

"Then the ship starts rising up from the plain. And I know it's being lifted by what's in the bags. The ship doesn't make any noise as it floats up into the sky. And when it does I can see past it to the rest of the plain, and the plain is covered with more of these silver ships, each with three round bags along the spine. Each one starting to float up into the sky. And none of this is making a sound. Hundreds of them. More than I can count. Going up.

"Up they go, all these silver ships. Higher and higher into the purple sky, until they get so far away all you can make out are these silver dashes. Hundreds of them. Thousands maybe. The whole purple sky sprayed with these silver flecks getting smaller and smaller.

"Then one of the flecks turns into a bright white spark and then another one does and the sky is all of a sudden filled with this twinkling. And there are trails of white behind the sparks. And I don't know why but it makes me feel very sad.

"I feel like maybe I should leave, go someplace, but I can't think of any place to go. Then, shreds start falling out of the sky all around me. Shreds I recognize as parts of the bags that lifted the ships, bits of the nets that secured them. All this discarded stuff, stuff they didn't need any more, spinning down and landing all around me.

"And then I woke up."

Ppp looked at me and I looked at Ppp. We didn't say anything. For a long time there was nothing but the sounds of the tripod mechanism, walking us across the Earth.

Ppp turned toward the quartz and so did I.

The dark-skinned and golden-eyed show up in your dreams sometimes. You're supposed to file a report when they do. No one ever does.

"They're in the scrolls," Ppp said without looking at me. "The ones with the golden eyes. At least they used to be. They were gone the last time I looked for them. In the scrolls."

"They revise the scrolls, you know that," I reminded him.

"I wonder about that, too," he said and reached in front of him and made a cross on the inside of the quartz with the tip of his dominant tentacle. "If the scrolls are ancient documents, the underpinning of Martian society, how can they go back in and change them? And who decides what gets changed?"

"I don't know," I said, trying to make it sound like "I don't care."

"But they used to be in there. The ones with the golden eyes."

"So what if they were? Now they're gone because nobody believes in them anymore. That's why they took them out."

"If they never existed, how come they show up in our dreams?"

I didn't want to answer him. Mostly because I didn't like him saying "our dreams." As if he knew I dreamed of them, too. As if dreaming about the dark-skinned ones with golden eyes was something everybody did at some point. Besides, it's nobody's business what I dream about.

We both jumped when Hhh gave the attention call from the point tripod. I grabbed the controls and turned to look through the streaked quartz.

There was Hhh in the lead, the third tripod beyond him off to the right. Ahead of us something a dull silver-gray color stretched out along the floor of the valley we were in. In front of one section of silver was a collection of dark boxes all tumbled together.

Hhh signaled for us to keep our separation as we moved closer.

The boxes became more distinct. They were buildings. All different sizes and colors. One was as tall as a tripod. It was narrow and came to a point and stood at the middle of . . . it was a nest, that's what it was. It was a place where the cardos nested. We could see dozens of cardos, stumbling along paths, swarming around the structure.

As we got closer, we could see what the silver was behind the nest. It was water, stretched out as if in a canal, but not in a canal. It wasn't something that had been engineered, it was water wandering through the valley and past the nest. There's a word for that. Rivers. They had them on Mars before things dried up and they had to build the canals.

But here on Earth, there's so much water on this planet it makes you dizzy. Water falling out of the sky, water spilling through the hills, water so wide we thought it was land. These stupid little cardos had more water than they could ever need. It didn't seem fair to me.

Hhh sounded "Prepare."

Yyy finally decided to join us under the cowl.

"What's going on? Where are we?"

I didn't feel like explaining, so I pointed through the quartz and let him figure it out for himself.

"What are those?" he asked and pointed at something at

the edge of the nest.

What he was pointing at was a cluster of tubes mounted on rolling platforms. There were cardos swarming around and behind the tubes. All dressed the same.

Cannons. More cannons.

A gout of fire unfolded from the front of one cannon and gray smoke grew at the rear. A moment later the ground in front of Hhh's lead tripod erupted from the impact of a projectile.

They were like the cannon we faced the other night. But these were much larger. The sound was louder, and they chewed up much more ground when their shells hit.

Hhh blasted "Disperse," and his tripod started moving forward with a weaving motion to keep the cannons from getting his range. I took us to the left, the far tripod went to the right.

Another cannon discharged and fell short in front of us and to the side as I leaned on the tripod controls and we ran faster around the far side of the nest.

"Charge the convectors, Yyy," I said.

"I guess I better," was his surprisingly indifferent response.

I was waiting for some tactical glyphics to show up on the repeater next to me, waiting for Hhh to tell me to find a target. I wasn't looking forward to setting fire to any more of these animals. I didn't want to know what it was like to watch them burn and run in daylight.

Hhh saved me from that.

I saw the risers of Hhh's tripod brace for recoil, then a clutch of canisters was lobbed from under the turret. They scattered in the air and fell near the weapons and in the nest, one colliding with the top of that tallest building, cracking it open. A large metal cup-shaped object that must have been suspended in the tower came tumbling out. It fell, making deep, hollow noises as it dropped and crashed.

Where the other canisters fell they broke open and plumes of black smoke climbed into the air. The smoke quickly fell back down, more like a liquid than a gas, and started oozing over the nest.

What I liked about the black smoke was that you didn't have to watch things die. The smoke killed what it found but covered what it was doing. And it was fast. I guess it wasn't as bad as burning.

The smoke filled the narrow gaps between the buildings and spilled over the places where the weapons were. They didn't have time to get off another shot. Nothing moved in the nest. Nothing made any noise. All in all, much better than using the convectors.

Hhh sent glyphics that we were to close up and follow the water to see where it led. Any more nests, we'd deal with them as we went.

Hhh went around the nest and walked his tripod into the water. We swung around and formed a tighter triangle with Hhh still at point. Yyy, Ppp, and I were on one bank of the water, the third tripod was on the opposite bank. I don't remember if I was ever told the names of the Martians in the third tripod. If I was, I've forgotten them.

We started through the valley.

•

The large nest was behind us and around a bend in the river when the condensed water vapor stopped falling. Drops and streaks clung to the quartz. There was still a gray blanket above us as we went through the valley, but we could see the sky ahead was clearing. Not blue, but brighter.

There were smaller nests along the banks of the natural canal. We could see little knots and clusters of cardos on the paths and in the nests, but Hhh signaled we shouldn't bother with them as long as they didn't throw anything at us.

Yyy stayed below the turret, sulking. Ppp was behind the bulkhead. He might have been resting, but I think he was worried that he'd told me about his dream. So I was by myself, keeping pace with Hhh as he waded his machine down the center of the flowing water.

There were constructions floating in the water. Not skimmers, but things that must have done the same job as skimmers. They had rudders and sails and front ends made to slice through water. Cardos must have made them. All this distance from Mars and they came up with something that looked like it would work on the canals. What are the odds of that happening? And those circles they use to get around. That's really very clever if you stop to think about it. We haven't come up with anything like that. Maybe we should start using that idea.

Objects like the machine Ppp and I saw on the metal pipes, maybe we should keep some of them around. For reference. Or put them in a museum. Put them in a museum with those small gold gear cases like the one I found. There are probably more of those about. When the invasion's finished it might be worth studying devices like that.

But Leadership probably wouldn't be interested in that suggestion. Tell the truth, I'm pretty sure Leadership would be against the concept of a museum that did anything other than honor all things Martian and victorious. And I don't think they'd be too happy with anybody who floated the idea.

Still, I was feeling sorry about throwing away the case with the gears and the springs. It scared me, but I should have kept it. As a reminder. A souvenir. Maybe I can pick up another one somewhere along the way.

·

The sky continued to get brighter, but never turned blue that day. It stayed a glaring, diffused white. The farther we went, the wider the natural canal became and the more nests we saw along the shore. There were some weapons thrown at us, smaller projectiles and now and then a stuttering spray of pellets like the ones that killed Qqq. But these were too far away to penetrate the tripod and clanged off when they hit. Hhh didn't bother with them, so we didn't either.

And then the water got even wider and we started to see what was ahead of us. The mouth of the canal kept opening until it was an expanse of water that came up to the second joint of the risers on Hhh's lead tripod. We stayed along the edge as long as we could, but we eventually had to move into the water or we would have gotten too much spread between us.

Then the water closed a little, into what you could call a channel, defined by tall rocks on either side. Past the rocks, it opened up again. And when it did, all three machines came to a stop on this narrow run of white sand, one after another, taking our lead from Hhh.

None of us had ever seen what was spread out under that white sky. None of us. Ahead was more water than I thought could exist anywhere in the universe. This planet was drowning in water. It stretched out to the horizon, where it edged up against the sky. And at the place where the sky met the water, there were shapes. A line of dark gray tubes and boxes floating on the horizon, each one trailing the kind of smoke that came from the cone on the land tube Ppp and I saw.

When we looked down from the horizon, we could see the water in front of us was crowded with floating boxes and tubes. They were like pieces of the cardo nests bobbing on the surface of all that water, like the skimmers I saw on the river, big ones and small ones, different shapes, some with sails, some with cones pumping their own smoke into the sky.

And on the boxes and tubes were hundreds of cardos. Probably thousands of them, teeming on board these floating contrivances. And you could hear them, even through the quartz. They made this collective noise, all those cardos. It was a garbled, fragmented moan of a sound. And the bigger floaters were making noise, too. The ones making smoke made something like the sound the land tube made.

Then they all started to move away from shore, scrambling across the surface. It was because they saw us standing at the edge of the water. They started crashing into each other and some of them were sinking and you could make out the foam where some of the cardos were thrashing around.

I looked over at Hhh's tripod and it was as if the machine

itself couldn't comprehend what it was looking at; the cabin and cowl moved slowly back and forth, like it was trying to make sense of it all. I think Hhh was getting ready to signal us to keep moving up the coast and leave this mob to itself.

That's when I looked up from the confusion close to shore and saw something cutting through the water faster than any of the other floaters, heading toward the beach. Hhh must have seen it the same moment I did because he leaned on the "Prepare" horn and added that noise to everything else that was going on.

What we saw was this enormous piece of metal. It was bigger, taller than any of the other floaters, churning through the water, black smoke pouring, blasting from two tremendous barrels on its back. It was wide and dark gray with a tower and some kind of rigging strung above the barrels. But what made me shake was what I saw on the front of the floater. Back from the end that was slicing through the water, and pushing the other floaters aside, was some kind of housing. And out of the housing poked two of the tubes the cardos used on us at the nest. Two more cannons. But these looked even bigger.

And as I watched I could see they were lifting higher, getting the range on us.

"Get us out of here, Vvv!"

I hadn't heard Yyy come up behind me, but there he was, yelling in my tympano.

"It looks like one of those metal engines on rails." Ppp was there, leaning against the quartz, looking at the dark gray beast. "But it's so much bigger."

"I know, I know," was all I could think to say. Now I had a sense of how Qqq must have felt when he took control of the tripod and sent us staggering into the darkness beyond the pit. That feeling of panic pushing everything else out of your brain.

"Get us OUT!" Yyy was shouting and beating me on the back of the head with his tentacles.

Hhh's tripod stepped deeper into the water, then I saw it brace ahead of the push of recoil. Then a clutch of canisters was thrown at the large floater.

They smashed against the side of the monster and burst, then bounced away trailing the black smoke.

"Convectors!" I shouted.

"Are you crazy?" Yyy shouted back.

"I'll charge them," Ppp called back as he went to the plates covering the pump shank.

When I had the big floater in range, I tripped the discharge. But my shot was low, missing the craft and burning a big steaming gash in the water in front of it. We lost sight of the floating engine in the smoke and mist from the boiling water. Then there was a hot orange ball inside the steam. The floater must have fired, but we couldn't tell in what direction.

The cabin and cowling of the tripod on the right flank exploded. Quartz and metal and flesh blossomed up into the air. There was nothing left but the risers, still under power and staggering out into the water.

"OUT, VVV. GET US OUT!"

Hhh discharged his convectors at the attacking floater and sliced through it at the midpoint. It ruptured and lobbed metal and smoke and cardos and fire into the air to form a burning halo. But it kept coming. It fired from one of the tubes, but the shot went past Hhh on one side and past us on the other. Hhh was lowering his convectors, but the damn thing was too close.

The remains of the big floater rammed into the forward riser of Hhh's machine. Nothing moved at first and I thought the tripod might have survived the impact. Then the riser buckled and, with what seemed a terrible slowness, the tripod crumpled forward and collapsed across the burning wreck of the floating war machine.

War Machine. That's what it was. It was more of a War Machine than the spindly farm equipment we were charging around in. Tripods are for harvesting. They use them to melt the ice caps and poison the cufor with the black smoke. That device, that metal monster coming out of the sea at us, that was a real War Machine. That was designed to kill anything that got in its way. And the cardos built it. Those tiny, chittering, flammable stick-figures built that nightmare. That one, and all those others lined up on the horizon. Built them and whatever else they had waiting for us on the other side of all that water.

The transparent, ripply dome of a shock wave expanded over all of us when the tripod and whatever was left in the War Machine exploded.

More metal, more steam, more blood.

"Now will you get us out of here?" Yyy was shaking me with his tentacles. "Now? Now?"

I turned around and slapped Yyy across the face, then I put the tip of my dominant tentacle up against his left eye.

"You touch me again, Yyy, and I will skewer you, and toss your body out of this machine. Do you understand me?"

Yyy focused on the tentacle I was about to shove through his brain. Neither one of us moved.

"Do you understand me, Yyy?"

Outside the tripod we could hear secondary explosions and the groaning complaint of collapsing metal and the bellowing horns of the other floaters heading out to sea.

We might still be there if Ppp hadn't whispered into Yyy's tympano, "I think you should tell him you understand."

"I understand," Yyy said without moving his lips.

I pulled back my tentacle. The three of us exhaled.

Then Yyy asked, in a very calm voice, "Can we go away from here now? Please."

"Yes, we can," I answered as calmly as he'd asked.

Yyy and Ppp left me alone at the controls. I turned the cabin on the turret and started the tripod away from the water.

Fortunately, neither one of them had asked me where we were going, because I had no idea about that whatsoever.

All I knew for sure was, in spite of all my best efforts, I was back in charge.

Book Two

The Earth Under The Martians

Yyy was making the noise again today. It's difficult to describe. I've never witnessed anything like it. You can see it coming. His eyes start to close and he stands still, as if something was trying to get his attention. His mouth drops open and he gasps in a big gulp of air and holds it. Then it all comes blasting back out of him. Fluid comes with it. Then he opens his eyes, but not all the way because there's a sticky film over them, some kind of secretion in the aftermath. Then he makes a damp snorting sound, like he's trying to pull something down his throat that's threatening to escape. It's not a pleasant sound.

He started doing this about the time we met up with Mmm. He did it once the first day, but now he's doing it so often I've lost count. I think Ppp is still counting. He's keeping the log. They asked us to keep a log. Mmm feels it's important for us to maintain an accurate record for the sake of history. Whatever Mmm wants us to do is fine with me. I've given all the orders I ever want to give.

If we hadn't found Mmm and his group I don't know what would have happened to us.

After we saw Hhh and the other tripod destroyed by the cardo War Machine, I took us inland until we couldn't see the water anymore. We weren't going anywhere. All we were doing was moving away from where we'd been.

Along the way we kicked over a big box of a structure. It was like turning over a rock. A hundred animals came running out, scattering in all directions. Cardos, four appendaged thoats, and more of those fluffy calots. They all must have been hiding in the structure.

Yyy pushed up to the quartz and started beating on it with his tentacles.

"Burn them!" he was shouting. "Burn them all, right now!"

Yyy's terror had retreated far enough for his anger to move forward. And, really, I understood him. I think for the first time I felt sorry for Yyy. This adventure was not working out at all the way he thought it would. And after what we saw at the edge of the water, I'll confess there was plenty of anger churning around inside me and I was ready to use the convectors to give Yyy what he wanted.

I don't know what stopped me, but something did. Not that I cared, but I was hungry and I didn't know how far we had to go. I didn't even know where we were going.

"We won't burn them," I said. "We'll catch them."

I looked at Yyy. He wasn't going to argue. He took over the articulators for the external tentacles and started picking up cardos and tossing them into the larder basket at the back of the cabin. He was none too gentle about how he went about it. Ppp didn't like this anymore than I did, but I wasn't going to say anything. It wasn't worth it. It wouldn't have accomplished anything.

So we fed off what Yyy caught, then tried to reason what we should do next.

Nobody liked the idea of us being on our own again. We knew what that was like and we knew what it felt like to have some organization, someone in charge who was used to being in charge, even if that didn't last long.

Maybe we could find another cylinder.

We switched on the beacon locator, but there was nothing in range. So we started moving and let the auto-stabilizer be in charge for a while, taking turns watching through the quartz and checking for beacons.

There wasn't any discussion, but we stayed clear of cardo nests. There were enough of them wandering over hills and fields we could pluck as needed. Wandering, running, the same way we were, I suppose.

If we heard any explosions or weapons, we went the other way.

After a couple of days of this I realized we were doing exactly what Yyy had suggested we do when we first walked away from the pit. I remember giving him a hard time about it, but that was before the floating War Machine. That was back when I figured we would probably be okay. Back when Hhh thought we could take care of ourselves and fulfill the mission.

Then Hhh got himself scattered to the winds.

I wanted us to be part of a plan. We didn't need to know exactly what the plan was, all we had to worry about was doing our part. But I was starting to think the invasion itself might not have been all that central to Leadership's plan. Certainly not the main objective. I think the plan was to get everybody stirred up about the invasion so they wouldn't have time to think about anything else.

The actual plans for the invasion seemed to consist entirely of: "Make a big show of throwing Martians at the Earth and see how that works out."

The funny thing, if you want to think of it as funny, was that while the invasion may not have been living up to expectations, there was one aspect of Mars that was doing surprisingly well on Earth.

We were three or four days into our wandering when Ppp was the first one to notice and point it out to me and

Yyy.

"Over there. What does that look like to you?"

We were all in the cabin when Ppp pointed at the crest of a hill over to our left. What he was pointing at was a rim of vibrant red tracing the curves and dips of the land.

"It looks like creeper," Yyy said.

And it did. It looked like the deep red ciliate we left behind on Mars. It's an inexpensive protein source for the cardos and something with enough intelligence to migrate on its own and hold the soil together.

I nudged the controls and we climbed the hill, moving closer to the rim of red. We got to the top of the hill and I stopped the tripod. The three of us stared at the slope for a long time. The other side of the hill was a blanket of gently swaying red. So was the valley beyond. There was a run of water at the floor of the valley, or what had been water but was now a rope of red.

"It is creeper," Yyy announced.

"How can it be creeper?" Ppp asked.

"We brought it with us," I said as I had the thought.

Ppp and Yyy looked at me.

"You know how that stuff is," I said, opening my tentacles to take in the red vista. "It gets in everywhere. There'd just have to be a little spec of it on a piece of equipment. Once it touched the ground it would spread. There might have been more than one contamination. We probably had some of it on us."

"Maybe the Leadership planned that we should bring it," Ppp suggested.

I flicked my dominant tentacle at the red waves in front of us. "Nobody planned this. Like everything else, it's just something that happened. But I bet somebody's taking credit for it."

"What are you talking about?" Yyy said, once more proving his inability to think past the end of his beak.

"You know how fast creeper grows," I told him. "If half the cylinders carried it, even the ones that crashed would be spreading it. I bet they're back on Mars watching the Earth turn red and telling everybody how well things are going."

I looked at Yyy, daring him to question my enthusiasm. He didn't. He turned and looked out over the red hill, the red stream, the red valley. We all looked at it, and we all ended up feeling the same nostalgic tug.

"It's sort of nice to see it here," Ppp said. "Makes you think of home."

Which it did.

I'm not sure how long we stayed there, watching the red creeper, but it was a good long time. Then I turned the tripod and we went on. But now we stayed close to the leading edge of the red creeper as it crawled across the landscape. I followed the creeper, as if it was going to lead us somewhere we wanted to go.

•

We moved with the edge of the red tide for, I think, four days. Then the communication tool picked up a beacon and we chased after it. There was nothing but a hole in the ground and an empty cylinder at the end of the beacon.

It was like that for the next two beacons we connected with. Nothing but empty wrecks covered with red creeper by the time we reached them. Maybe the red creeper would end up doing the conquering for us.

Moving away from the third crash site, we came upon some cardos and tossed them in the larder. It looked like they'd started eating the red creeper. That made sense. That's what we were feeding them at home.

•

I was at the controls, even though they were on auto-stabilize, set to follow the edge of the red creeper. If I wasn't there, Yyy would want to be there, and I didn't like the idea of him being anywhere near the controls. There was no moon that night. The sky was swarming with stars, so sharp, so clear, you could understand why our ancestors believed they were just out of reach.

"Can you see home?"

I turned and saw Ppp behind me, facing the quartz and looking at the stars.

I searched the correct quadrant of the sky and found a dot with the faintest flicker of red to it.

"Yes. It's there," I said and pointed at the dot. "Forty degrees up from the horizon, to the edge there."

I looked at him, at his open face, as he stared at the place we came from. Beneath us the tripod risers trudged on, uninterested in where they were taking us.

"If we fail, everyone at home will die. Won't they?"

"Everyone at home will die anyway," I said.

Ppp turned to look at me and, I don't know, something about the way he looked at me made me ashamed of what I'd said.

"You know, I'm not stupid," he said.

"I didn't say you were stupid."

"I know everybody's going to die eventually. But you make it sound like that's a reason not to do anything. Maybe you're the stupid one."

Maybe I am.

"I'm sorry, Ppp. Sometimes it's like I've got this reflex and I can't do anything about it. Whatever somebody says, I feel I have to smack it away, like I had to protect myself."

"From what?"

"I don't know."

"Don't you want Mars to keep going?"

"I guess I do. I mean, I suppose so. But it doesn't seem to have a lot to do with me. I don't feel I've got much of a stake in the outcome. Personally. You know what I mean?"

Ppp's look had softened and I was grateful for that. I didn't like the idea of Ppp being mad at me.

"I guess I do," he said looking out at the sky.

Neither one of us said anything for awhile. Then, for no real reason I could say, I flipped off the auto-stabilizer and took the controls and brought the tripod to a halt. The risers stopped their metal rhythms of bending, extending, contracting, bending, extending, contracting. The cabin grew quiet, except for the ticking of the metal as the power plant cooled below us.

Ppp and I, we looked at the stars.

After a long time Ppp said out loud what he must have been thinking about for a very long time.

"They're different. The cardos here. They're sort of like the ones on Mars and the ones they found on Venus, but they're different. I mean, they build things."

"That they do," I said without looking at him. "That they most certainly do."

"How'd they learn to do that? Who taught them to do that?"

"Beats me."

"Maybe we could figure out a way to get along with them."

"What?"

"I don't know, share the planet."

"Share the planet while we're eating them? I don't see that going over big with the cardos."

"I guess not."

"Ppp, they're inferior. You can't forget that," I think I was saying that as much for myself as I was for Ppp. Maybe more.

"But look what they've made. The machines and the big nests and the floater that got Hhh and the others."

"Maybe they didn't built that stuff after all. Maybe somebody gave it to them and they use it."

"Like we use the things we've got without knowing how we got them?"

"I don't think that's the same thing," I said even though it sounded exactly like the same thing.

Ppp let that one slide. We listened to the convector chamber cycle and vent, as if the tripod had been listening to what we were talking about and decided to contribute a sigh.

Then, based on nothing we'd been discussing, Ppp asked me, "How old are you, Vvv?"

"How old am I? I don't know. Old enough. Not as old as some. Older than a lot."

"Did you ever bud?"

"No, I never saw much point to it."

"They make it sound like a responsibility. You know, to keep the species going."

"It's not something I ever wanted to do."

"How come?"

"This is getting kind of personal, Ppp."

"I don't think I'm going to. It doesn't seem fair. To the bud, I mean. Under the circumstances."

"If Martians stop budding, there won't be any more Martians, and that brings us right back to where we started. Keeping the species going."

"Why?" Ppp said, asking the question Hhh warned me about asking.

"Why? Because somebody's got to keep the lights on," I told him.

"Who asked us to?" Ppp said, moving on to another awkward question. "Who said we could do whatever we want to do to keep life going? How do we know if we're doing it right? I mean, we move and we live and then we stop. Did you ever wonder why?"

I hadn't given much thought to these questions. Certainly not before we got to this wretched planet. Now that I'm here, now that it's too late to do much of anything about the situation, I can't stop thinking about the whys and the whos.

"I think it's supposed to be about what we do between the time we bud and the time we stop," I said. "How we fill up the space."

I looked past Ppp to the sky and the stars. And I felt myself filling up with emptiness. An emptiness that took up all the space inside me.

How old am I?

"I wish I was on the Tirra," I heard myself saying.

"What?"

"I said I wish I was on the Tirra Canal right now and not here."

"Oh," Ppp said.

We looked at the stars some more, then Ppp half turned around and looked at me out of the circumference of his eye.

"Cardos don't bud, right?" I couldn't tell if Ppp was changing the subject or forgot what we were talking about.

"They're primitive animals, Ppp. They don't bud because they can't. They do something different to get more cardos. Didn't anybody ever tell you about how cardos happen?"

"Oh, sure, I know about that. I mean how there's two kinds of cardos and you have to fit them together to grow more. And they grow inside one of the two kinds of cardos. And it's always the one type of cardo that grows them inside, they don't take turns or anything like that. And they're still growing when they fall out so it takes a while till you can start feeding from the new ones. I know all that. It's just . . . "

"Just what?"

Ppp's face scrunched up into a crinkly representation of thought.

"What does that even look like?"

"Don't ask me. I'm from the big city."

A scratch of green light moved across the sky. It came from behind us and arced a little to one side before disappearing below the horizon.

"Reinforcements," Ppp whispered.

"Let's hope so," I said as I powered up the tripod and started chasing after the falling star.

On the other side of the bulkhead, Yyy was asleep in his hammock. That was the first time we heard him make that funny, wet, expulsion of a sound.

•

It was the middle of the next day when we reached the freshly fallen cylinder. It had landed beyond the edge of the red creeper. They'd opened the cap and were assembling their first tripod when we reached the top of a hill and saw them. Ppp made a gasping sound when we saw at least ten Martians working around the cylinder. Yyy didn't say anything, but I could feel him trembling next to me. It had been so long since we'd seen so many Martians in a group . . . alive.

"Ulla!" went up from the new arrivals.

We answered, "Ulla!" and raced toward them.

Mmm was in charge. He wanted an immediate report, which we gave him. We were getting to the part of the story where we joined Hhh and followed his group to the edge of the water and what happened there when I realized the rest of Mmm's crew had stopped work and were squatting quietly in a semicircle behind us. Listening.

I thought maybe we'd screwed up so badly we were going to be punished. Mmm must have seen the look on my face.

"They're curious," he said.

"Curious about what happened?" I asked.

"No, curious about you. You were in The First Cylinder. You were the vanguard. They admire you. They envy you. All we can do now is follow. You will always be the first."

Poor frightened Qqq. He was right. The first is the one

who'll be remembered.

"Which one of you was the first out of the cylinder?" Mmm asked. "Who was the first Martian to touch the surface?"

I looked at Mmm. Then I looked at the other freshly landed Martians. Then I looked at Ppp and Yyy. I was the first. I didn't touch the surface, I smacked my face against it, but I was the first. I was History.

I turned to Mmm, swallowed, then I said, loud and clear, "Qqq was the first one out, the first one on the ground. He took over when Ddd was killed and led us to safety. Qqq unscrewed the cap and went out ahead of us. Qqq was the first Martian on Earth."

"It was Qqq," Ppp said to my right.

"It was Qqq," Yyy said to my left.

Mmm and the rest of his crew struggled against gravity to rise as tall as they could and saluted Qqq with a great and prolonged ululation.

We pulled cardos from the larder and toasted the courage of Qqq, the first Martian on the surface of the Earth. It was a very enthusiastic celebration.

•

Mmm and I left Ppp and Yyy telling the newcomers about our adventures. We moved some distance from the landing site, up a hill where we could look down on the others and the freshly assembled tripod standing next to the battle-scarred one we arrived in. We were at the leading edge of the red creeper which grew so fast you could almost sit there and watch it move down the hillside, watch it claim the Earth for itself. If a stupid vegetable can do that, what was our problem?

Mmm turned his back on the camp. I looked down. He was standing on red creeper, I was standing on the green vegetation that grows here.

"I'll be honest with you, Vvv," Mmm said. "Your finding us, essentially welcoming us to this hostile world, has made a tremendous difference to the crew. I confess, it's made a difference to me as well. To meet the Martians who led this invasion, well . . . It's been an almost immeasurable boost to morale."

"You're welcome, sir, I guess. But honestly, we're not heroes. Except for Qqq. If anybody deserves a statue, it's Qqq." I said, and I meant it.

"Yes, well, there'll be time enough for statues when this is over. And it'll be over soon, I believe. Certainly this aspect of the operation will be over. One way or the other."

"One way or the other?"

Mmm laced his tentacles together in front of him and rotated them, one around another, in contemplation.

"It shames me to say this, Vvv, but I fear home support for the invasion has eroded considerably since those first heady days when you set off on your quest."

"We heard there were some problems."

"Yes, problems and setbacks and a certain amount of second guessing. The population was promised much and sacrificed much, but events have not manifested themselves as positively as we had all wished."

"Hhh said there had been protests."

"Officially there have been no protests. Which means any protests are unofficial, and unofficial events don't exist. Officially. The tribunals helped for a while, but then the tribunals themselves became a source of friction. When you get citizens all fired up about something and then it doesn't work out exactly as planned, you have to anticipate a certain level of disappointment to infect the community. Once the public gets a thought into its collective head, it can be exceedingly recalcitrant about letting go and moving on."

"If you don't mind my asking, what does 'moving on' look like under current conditions?"

"Good question, Vvv. Which brings me to an additional level of allegory informing our meeting here so far away from home. For while you and your companions were the first to reach the Earth, my crew and I have piloted what will be, for an indeterminate period, the last cylinder launched."

"I don't think that actually constitutes an allegory."

"Oh, well, I may have meant irony. I often get the two confused."

"Are you telling me they're calling off the invasion?"

"No, not calling it off. Rather, for the time being Leadership has decided to transition to a more tactically conservative phase of the operation."

"Which will consist of what?"

"Another excellent question, Vvv. While Leadership engages in a series of fact-finding investigations to consider all feasible options, the forces deployed here on Earth will consolidate and maintain."

"Consolidate what? Maintain how?"

"As you know from what Hhh told you, several cylinders did not arrive when and where they were supposed to. Other cylinders experienced difficulty landing and were damaged to one degree or another, their crews often decimated, as was the case with you and your craft. Adding to these issues, local resistance of a much more robust nature than anticipated has been encountered. All this has greatly increased the overall cost of the endeavor, straining budgets and tempers, disrupting schedules. This has resulted in certain key Leadership figures being confronted by highly partisan and, in my personal opinion, very rude questions. In light of the rapidly developing situation, certain temporary economizing schemes have been put in place. There is a substantial amount of salvageable material inside those damaged cylinders. What we are charged with, and by extension you and your tripod, is the locating, assessment, collection, and refurbishment of these resources so that we will be able to maintain an effective occupying force and continue to control the indigenous population."

I'd grown numb through most of what Mmm was saying. At first I couldn't really understand, then I started to unpack the meaning behind all the language. We were supposed to scavenge the battlefield for anything worth repairing because there would be no subsequent investment in our mission for "an indeterminate period." Understanding turned into anger.

"No more cylinders?" I shouted, startling Mmm. "No relief forces?"

"Let's keep it down, Vvv. You asked questions, I answered them. We have to work together to keep this unit operational."

I looked down the hill at the Martians. How many of us were on this planet?

We were expected to terrorize the cardo population, wreck all the nests we found, and stop them from building more War Machines. We could do that for a while, but we couldn't do it forever. Eventually the cardos were going to figure out what was going on. How long before they get over the shock of what's been happening and start organizing?

We'd started with surprise and violence, all we had now was violence. We were good at that, but it's not much by way of a plan.

Mmm was still talking to me.

"Of course, I'm telling you this in confidence, Vvv. I haven't shared any of what I've told you with my crew. I expect you'll want to do likewise with your lot. Less complicated."

"You mean I should lie to them," I said.

Not only was Mmm unclear on the difference between allegory and irony, he was apparently unfamiliar with sarcasm.

"Oh, no, you don't have to lie to them," he counseled me. "Just don't tell them the truth."

Mmm told me they had detected a nonresponsive cylinder within a two-day journey from where we were. He thought that would be a good place for me to start. After a night's rest and resupplying, we were to start on our new mission in the morning.

Mmm and I started down the hill, back toward our crews. Our intrepid and ignorant crews.

•

It took us more than two days to reach the cylinder. Yyy continued to have his wet eruptions. His eyes were coated with a gooey film and he was tired all the time. The second night Ppp fell down the access ramp to the servos. He said he felt dizzy and lost his grip. Me, I was feeling okay. Except the front of my head hurt. I know that's from staying at the controls more than I should.

I considered telling Ppp and Yyy what Mmm said about the situation back home. I didn't like carrying that around on my own, but it wouldn't do them any good to know. I expected the volume and frequency of Yyy's complaining would increase if I told him, and that was something none of us needed.

When we finally got to the coordinates, we found the cylinder rammed nose first into the ground having smashed through a structure at the edge of a fairly large cardo nest. Everything was frosted with red creeper.

The three of us looked down from the cabin at the shallow crater and the structure the cylinder had cracked open.

"Look at how they live," this from Ppp. He was no more amazed than Yyy and me. It was the first time any of us had been this close to a nest, let alone to one of the separate structures making them up. The first thing we noticed was that they were separate. From a distance we'd assumed all the boxes and covertures were connected. Something like a hive. At home we kept cardos in common spaces, usually with a roof and movable walls. If you were wealthy you could afford the price of unrestricted cardos, ones that were allowed to wander in large fenced-in tracts until they were herded in for distribution and consumption.

But this broken place we were looking at was self-contained, unattached to the boxes on either side of it. It had levels with what looked like segmented ramps connecting them.

"Is that someplace where they can roost?" Yyy was pointing at a flat rectangle balanced on four rods. There were four or five smaller assemblies of sticks, each attached to a small square with a brace coming up one side.

"Vvv," Ppp whispered. "I think that's a private shelter."

"Don't be crazy," Yyy snapped, then snorted back something glutinous that was collecting in his throat. "Cardos don't live in private shelters."

"Maybe they do here," Ppp said.

"Why would they do that?" Yyy asked.

"Because they can. Because they're like us that way," Ppp said this cautiously, as if the idea was fragile or dangerous. Or both.

"Tell him he's crazy, Vvv."

Yyy expected me to back him up on this. I couldn't do it. Not after what I'd seen the cardos here could pull off. Maybe he was desperate for someone to say something to stop him from thinking what it would mean if these animals liked houses and rooms.

"That must be a table," Ppp said, pointing at the rectangle. "So, those must be what they use for slings and hammocks."

"Shut up!"

I got between Ppp and Yyy.

"Let's everybody shut up," I said. "We have to get that cylinder clear and open it. Let's take a look before it gets dark."

I eased the tripod down on its risers so we could climb out and see what we were up against.

We scraped some of the red creeper off the cylinder where it was stuck in the ground. It was buried not that far below the screw, but stuck fast. We weren't going to be able to rock it out; we'd have to dig down around it so we could get some leverage.

From the ground we could better see inside what was

left of the cardo shelter. Multiple levels with separate compartments, fabric covering the floors, arches and the metal frame of something that might have been for lighting.

There were shelves filled with what looked at first like bricks. Some of them had fallen off the shelves and were open. They weren't bricks. They were stacks of that scroll material, pressed together between stiff rectangles. The rectangles were wrapped in the same hide as the folder I found on the cardo where we crashed.

Yyy picked up one of the stacks and shook it back and forth between his tentacles. The sheets made a thin flapping noise as they fluttered between the hard covers. The noise amused Yyy. The corners of his mouth curled up into a grin.

Yyy's pleasures in life were very simple ones.

He looked at the sheets flipping by then suddenly stopped. He turned to me, his smile gone, and said, "No."

"'No' what?" I asked.

He held the large folder open for me to look at.

"These can't be glyphics. They can't be."

I looked at what he was holding.

Sheets and sheets of the scroll material, bound together, suggesting permanence. And all covered with regiments of squiggles like the ones I found on the tiny scrolls in the folder that belonged to the dead cardo.

Squiggles. Countless squiggles. On both sides. The squiggles were bigger at the front of the folder. None of them made sense to me.

THE
PIAZZA TALES

BY
HERMAN MELVILLE

AUTHOR OF "TYPEE," "OMOO," ETC.,
ETC., ETC.

NEW YORK;
DIX & EDWARDS, 321 BROADWAY
LONDON: SAMPSON LOW, SON & CO.
1856

"Leave it," I said and threw it aside.

"But if those are glyphics . . . "

"Aren't you tired, Yyy? I know I am."

Yyy looked back, looked at all the scattered folders full of thin sheets of scroll material. Hundreds of them, on the shelves and on the floor.

"Yeah. I'm tired."

We left the shelter and went back to the tripod. Nobody felt like eating.

●

"Did you hear that?" Ppp had stopped digging and was facing the crushed shelter.

"Hear what?" I asked him.

"I thought I heard something. Something in the shelter."

"You heard something falling down in there. The whole place will probably come down when we push the cylinder."

"It didn't sound like something falling. It sounded like something alive. A noise. Like an animal."

I stopped where I was and listened.

"I hear the wreckage groaning," I said.

"No, it wasn't the shelter. It was like an animal."

"Maybe that's what it is. Something got caught when the shelter was hit."

Ppp kept standing there. I really didn't have the patience for this. I was tired and my head hurt and Yyy was up in his hammock resting, so it was the two of us digging out the cylinder.

"Come on, Ppp. This is already taking too long. Dig."

I went back to digging. Ppp listened a little longer, then came around to my side of the cylinder to help.

•

Yyy had found a different noise to make. A new sound to add to a growing collection of moist, gassy expulsions. Now when he slept his mouth hung open and served as an echo chamber for a wet, ragged rasping that went with every breath. It would have woken me up if I'd ever managed to get to sleep, which I hadn't.

I climbed out of the hammock and pushed against my closed eyes with my tentacles. It felt like my head was filling with a pressurized liquid that sloshed around inside me whenever I moved, pushing against the back of my eyes, threatening to push them clean out of their sockets.

I looked to see if Ppp was asleep, but his hammock was empty.

I went to the cabin and looked out and saw Ppp, shiny gray in the moonlight, settled on the ground, looking into the darkness of the wrecked shelter.

I climbed down from the tripod and moved to stand behind Ppp as he stared into the debris.

"What are you doing out here?"

Ppp turned around at the sound of my voice. He didn't seem surprised to see me. "Oh, hi, Vvv. I'm listening."

"Listening to what?"

"Listening to the shelter. Or whatever is in there. I think it's more under than in it. I think it's trapped. I don't think it can get out unless we help."

"There's nothing in there, Ppp."

"Listen for a minute. You'll hear it."

He turned away from me to face the broken shelter again and leaned forward to give it his full attention. I was in no rush to go back to the tripod and listen to Yyy's festival of gargles and gasps, so I settled down next to Ppp.

The night was cool. The moon was high and reached into the crushed shelter to paint everything a hard bluish white. You could hear the beams complaining and random bits of glass falling, but nothing that sounded like it was trapped.

I wanted to tell Ppp what I knew about Mars, how we were on our own for "an indeterminate period." I was tired of carrying that around by myself. Telling him wouldn't change anything, but I thought at least I might feel a little less alone.

"Hear that?" Ppp whispered.

"No."

"Listen harder."

I listened harder. Another piece of plaster. The dirt shifting under the cylinder behind us. Then I heard something else. A faint whine that wasn't being made by the shattered structure.

"Ezjuzt," is what I heard. Then, "O Gawd. Ezjuzt. Ezjuzt."

"There! I told you," Ppp said, curling one tentacle and lifting it in satisfaction.

"Gawd, woah faallee."

"You're right, Ppp. There's something trapped down there. Probably trapped since the crash."

"Poor thing must be frightened. And hungry."

"Reephant. Reephant."

"It's a language, isn't it, Vvv? It's how they communicate with others of their kind."

"Yeah, I think so. Like the squiggles in all those folders." I was thinking out loud, thinking thoughts I'd been avoiding. Like how the Earth cardos must have something like a language, a language they could set down and distribute. The ability to make War Machines and weapons like the ones we'd seen wasn't something you could pass down through oral tradition.

"The squiggles are the noises they make written down?"

"Could be."

"Ah-preecisors oh ta puur et kneehe."

"Maybe we could figure out how to talk to them," Ppp said. I looked at him and could see his brain was charging way ahead of the situation and the resources. "If we could talk to them we could work something out. Maybe."

"Maybe."

"We've got to get it out, dig it out of there. If we free it, it'll know we're friendly."

"Ppp, don't get your hopes up."

Ppp looked at me and I could see in the moonlight all that was holding him together was hope. Then his body shook as a chill ran along his tentacles and he made one of the raspy noises Yyy had started to make.

"Ta ynn pess o Gawd!"

•

Something's happening to us. None of us seem to have any

stamina. None of us can complete any physical task without stopping once, twice, or more to catch our breath. That's why it took till after sunrise to move the tripod and resettle it so the exterior tentacles were in a position where they could reach into the wreckage.

We didn't hear any sounds as we were working and I thought there was a good chance whatever was in there had died while we were panting and moving equipment. But as we were getting ready to climb back into the cabin and activate the tentacles, we heard the weak, senseless voice coming from what we figured to be an underground part of the crushed structure.

"Wooah untooth zis oonfatefool cette! Wooah."

"It's still alive," Ppp cried and was the first back into the tripod.

"Who cares?" Yyy wheezed.

Back under the cowling, Ppp went to the articulators for the exterior tentacles and started manipulating them. Yyy and I stood behind him and watched the metal appendages uncoil from under the turret and reach toward the smashed shelter.

With one tentacle Ppp held up a section of flooring and guided the other one under the structure. At first the microphone in the tip didn't pick up any sounds except the tentacle pushing aside bits of rubble. Then we heard the voice coming over the cabin speakers.

"Iiii ave bensteel tol ong."

"Okay, hang on, we're coming for you." This Ppp

whispered to himself as he worked the actuators.

All Yyy and I could see through the quartz was the section of the tentacles leading from the tripod into the wreckage. With the responders in his controls, Ppp had a replicated sense of what the tentacles were feeling as they explored. So we stopped looking through the quartz and watched Ppp's face for a sense of what he was finding.

The voice grew clearer. Ppp followed the sound with the tentacles.

"Wooah untooth zis oonfatefool sitte!"

"I'm close," Ppp told us. "I can feel the air moving around down there."

Then the voice again, loud this time. The tentacle must have been very close to it.

"Himahs boore vitneece!"

The voice stopped, and there was what sounded like something scrambling over the debris. It almost sounded as if there were two animals down there and they were fighting. Maybe it was the one and it panicked when it saw the tentacle. Some more of this, then it was quiet. Ppp swept the tip of the tentacle back and forth, listening, feeling.

Then . . .

"I've got something," Ppp said. He moved the actuators, and we watched the sensations of what it was touching move Ppp's face. "It feels like an appendage."

"Can you get a grip on it?" I asked.

"I think so."

Ppp twisted his own tentacles linked to the exterior tools

through the actuators. It was like watching someone tying an invisible knot.

"Got him!"

"Pull him out," I said. "Take your time, try not to hurt it."

"I won't, I won't."

Yyy's body shook with another spasm. Spittle flew out of his mouth and sprayed across the inside of the quartz.

Ppp carefully retracted the exterior tentacles. I know I told him to be careful, but he moved the tentacles at a painfully slow rate. Finally, his prize arrived at the lifted part of the flooring. He pulled it up and held it in front of the cabin quartz.

Ppp had the thing by its hind appendages and was holding it upside down. It was wrapped in dark fabric, oddly shaped and not very large. It wasn't moving, aside from the gentle swing it performed at the end of the tentacle.

Behind me, Yyy started to laugh. The laugh turned into a soggy croaking and ended with him saying, "All that trouble for this?"

"Set it down," I told Ppp. "We'll go out and see if it's still alive."

Ppp gently put the cardo down on the ground in front of the tripod and unwrapped the tentacle from the thing. We probably should have waited till we got out there to do that. Ppp disengaged himself from the actuators and we all climbed out to examine the body.

The three of us formed a triangle around the trophy Ppp had pulled from the wreckage. The cardo was alive; we could see the torso rise and fall. It was very oddly shaped for a cardo. Rounder. Softer. There were blotchy red areas all over its face. It had no hair except for wisps around the back of the head.

"I think it's dying," Yyy said and poked its midsection with the end of a tentacle. The tip sank into the soft flesh. Yyy pulled his tentacle away and shook it, as if to shake off some contamination. "What do you want to do with it?" Yyy asked me.

I turned to Ppp. He was looking down at the cardo, its roundness increasing and decreasing as it breathed. Poor Ppp. He hadn't thought much past the idea of getting it free from the shelter.

"Well, I guess we could try to communicate with it. You know?"

Yyy snorted, the snort turning into one of his wet gargling noises. "Communicate? Sure," he said. "I'll tell you one thing. I think there's something really wrong with this one. It doesn't look good. Whatever we do, I'm not going to eat this one. It's gone bad. Look at it. Blown up like that and splotchy. That thing is spoiled."

I don't know what Ppp was hoping for, but he was clearly disappointed by how this was turning out. I felt sorry for him. None of us belonged here, but maybe Ppp belonged least of all. He wasn't bad, he was immature. They release these young buds way too early. They don't know how life works. Not that any of the rest of us do. Except, the older you get, the better you get at pretending you do.

"What do you want to do with it, Ppp?" I asked.

Ppp looked at me. He was looking at me for an answer. The ones like Ppp have got all the questions, but none of the answers.

Ppp moved his lips, as if he thought that would make words magically appear in his head and fall out on the ground. This did not occur.

Part of me wanted to slap him hard across the eyes. Look around, bud, see where you are, what you're up against. Stop dreaming.

"All right," I said. "Move it over in the shade. We still have to get this cylinder open. It won't take much to shove it over now."

"Let's get this over with," Yyy said and moved to get his tentacles around the cardo.

That's when the tiny eyes of the animal shot as open as they could and looked straight up at Yyy. The cardo opened its mouth and started to scream. A long, piercing note, not even close to a word. It squeezed the noise out of itself until it ran out of breath, then it filled its lungs and did it again.

Yyy stumbled back as the cardo got to its hind appendages, tripping over Yyy's tentacles and falling on top of him, screaming in Yyy's face. Yyy started slapping at the terrified animal with all his tentacles at once.

"Get it off me! Get it off me!" Yyy was yelling.

Ppp got behind the bloated cardo and started pulling it off Yyy. It came around on Ppp and dragged the tips of its pseudos across the lens of his right eye. Now Ppp was screaming and pushing the terrified animal away, trying to protect his eyes.

The beast wasn't attacking, it was panicking. Yyy rolled away from it. Ppp had fallen backwards and couldn't see. The soft cardo stood there, screaming. It was ugly and loud, and the way it screamed managed to make the insides of my head hurt even more.

I picked up a piece of a beam from the shelter and started after the thing. I was going to stop that screaming. That was the one thought in my head. No more screaming, please.

The cardo saw me coming, turned and fell in the dirt next to the cylinder. Then it started crawling away, all the time screeching, stabbing the inside of my head.

"Shut up!" I yelled at it, as if the animal could understand what I was saying.

It backed away from me, against the cylinder, fell and crawled around the far side. We'd done a better job clearing the tip of the cylinder than I thought we had. The cylinder started to move, shaking off dirt as it began to fall, putting the cardo in its shadow.

The cylinder fell. There was nothing any of us could have done to stop it. All we could do was watch it happen. The cardo looked up at the cylinder, saw it coming, but there wasn't enough time to get out of the way and no place to run even if there had been. It opened its mouth and pulled in all the air it could, preparing for one last scream. But the scream stayed inside its sad little body as the cylinder fell and crushed it.

In so doing, the tip of the cylinder came clear of the ground.

I dropped the beam I was holding and rolled over on my side. I was looking into the smashed shelter and listening to the three of us breath. There used to be so much air, but lately we were all having trouble getting it inside, pulling it in.

We rested where we fell. Three points of the same triangle that surrounded the cardo, now farther apart. I like triangles. I like threes. I don't know why, but there's something about three that I find very comforting.

I don't know how long we stayed like that before we silently agreed to crawl back into the tripod. We still had to open the cylinder, take out what was left of the crew, and salvage what equipment we could, but we wouldn't be able to do that now. Not for a while. The cardo was crushed under the cylinder, so it wasn't going anywhere. We crawled into the tripod, none of us saying anything, and climbed back into the hammocks.

•

In the dream I was in my skimmer on the Tirra Canal and I could see the sun striking the crystal cities in the sharp, young Ylla Mountains ahead, sending clean light back at me. The light hits the surface of the canal and turns into smaller shards of light that dance on the sail of the skimmer. Up ahead, around the turn, there's black smoke rising into the purple sky. Black smoke coming from something moving toward me on the canal.

I watch the black smoke, billowing as it rises and blending with the sky. Then the object that's making the smoke comes around the bend in the canal and I can see what it is. It's the cardo floating War Machine. The one that killed Hhh and his crew and then blew up. And, remarkably, I'm not afraid of it. I'm not even surprised to see it on Mars.

The War Machine comes toward me. They run up bright pennants in the rigging. I can hear them snapping in the breeze. And there's movement on the deck, figures on the deck. Martians. The deck of the cardo ship is crowded with Martians. They hold flags and pennants in their tentacles and wave them at me because they're glad they've finally found me.

I climb up the mast of the skimmer and I wave back at

the Martians on the cardo ship because I'm as happy to be found as they are to find me.

I call "Ulla" to them. And they all call "Ulla" back to me.

Then I hear Ppp calling "Ulla" and I'm back in my hammock. Not someplace I want to be, but that's where I am.

I looked over at Ppp. He was talking in his sleep. Saying "Ulla." Saying it as if he was calling to someone. Saying it the way I was saying it in my dream, calling to the Martians on the cardo floating War Machine.

It was as if we'd been having the same dream, Ppp and I. I didn't know that was possible.

•

We unscrewed the cap from the cylinder and found the crew dead inside, which is what I thought we'd find. The surprise was further back in the cylinder, in the hold. It was empty. No tripods, no spare parts, nothing. They sent this cylinder with nothing in it but Martians and a couple of cardos. They blasted them at the Earth with nothing they'd need once they got here.

"Somebody must have made a mistake," Ppp suggested.

Yyy and I looked at each other. We were too tired to explain to Ppp that there'd been way more than one mistake and they'd all happened long before we cracked open this particular cylinder.

We removed the bodies of the crew, anointed them with distillate, burned them, read from the scrolls, then scattered the ashes. We didn't bother pulping the cardos; we left them in the cylinder. It was getting dark by then so I said we should rest, get some sleep, and head back in the morning.

Nobody said anything about what we might be heading back to.

•

The oversized sun was almost directly overhead when we finally got underway the next day. So much for leaving in the morning.

We dragged ourselves into the cabin and set the auto-stabilizer to take us back the way we came to Mmm and his group. Ppp and Yyy went back to their hammocks once we got started. I stayed in the command sling behind the controls, watching them respond to instructions from the auto-stabilizer. I told myself I didn't want Yyy sneaking up here and taking the controls. But that wasn't true. At least not completely. Mainly I stayed behind the quartz because I felt slightly better when I was upright than when I was swaying in my hammock.

Stretched out in the hammock, the internal sloshing sensation was worse. I felt like I was drowning from the inside. I'd never felt like that on Mars.

The red creeper covered everything as far as I could see. And it was getting deeper. In the valleys the risers of the tripod would sometimes sink down to their second flex before the tread found solid ground. Swirling tides of red creeper. I was pretty sure it covered most of the planet by then. And the way it loved water I bet it started crawling out over those blue expanses the landing strategists thought were lava.

I admit there was something comforting . . . well, almost comforting . . . to think about this whole wretched muck ball turning bright, bright Martian red. I don't know what difference it makes if a planet is red or blue or covered in rotating Jovian stripes. None, I suppose.

But I suggest it's better to look at them and stay a safe distance away. Let them spin unmolested in their orbits. The trouble comes when you start going to all those pretty planets and find out there's life on them. When you think your planet is unique, the only one with creatures that can get up and move around, you feel special. Like you're responsible for representing the best of the universe. As if you were chosen for greatness and immortality and a bustling economy.

Mars was like that. A long time ago. Before the great disillusionment. Venus. You can't see your tentacle in front of your face on the surface of Venus. Nobody thought there was anything alive there. Makes you wonder, if they thought that why did they bother going? Science. Exploration. Plant the flag.

Lucky for us the inhabitants turned out to be edible so the enterprise could be justified.

Should have left well enough alone, if you ask me. But nobody asked me.

•

"I've been thinking."

Again, not something that bodes well coming from Yyy.

I heard him struggle into the cabin and come up behind

me late in the second day of trudging back to Mmm and the others. I wondered if they'd had any surprises like ours.

"About what, Yyy?" I really have to watch it with Yyy. As much as he gets on my nerves, I don't want to get him angry at me. Not that he could do anything about it, the condition he's in. But, hell, we're all pretty much in the same condition now.

"About what's happening to us."

"Such as?"

"Did you ever feel like this on Mars?"

"What do you mean, 'like this'?"

"Come on, Vvv. You know what I mean. We can barely move we're so tired, and there's always something burning in my throat, like it was full of something broken and hot. I never felt like this on Mars. Did you ever feel like this on Mars?"

"No."

"Did you ever know anybody who felt like this on Mars?"

"No."

"Did you ever even so much as hear of anybody feeling like this on Mars?"

"No."

"Well, that's what I'm saying."

"Saying what, Yyy?"

"Like I said about that squishy, round cardo back there. It didn't look right. There was something wrong with it. And what I've been thinking is they're doing it on purpose."

"Who's doing what on purpose, Yyy?"

"The Earth cardos. I think they're doing something to themselves so we'll get sick when we eat them."

"What, like they're poisoning us?"

"Exactly," he said, and coughed up a big yellow glob of

something from his lungs for emphasis.

"You think they're poisoning themselves in order to poison us? That's crazy."

"They're getting desperate," he said as if that settled the question.

"I don't know, Yyy. You're making some big leaps with this."

"Do you have a better explanation?"

"I don't have any explanation at all, but the idea that a population of food stock . . . "

"Really smart food stock," Yyy amplified, lifting the tip of a tentacle and pointing it upward.

"Okay, the idea that even really smart food stock, capable of doing what we've seen since we got here, that these creatures would decide the best way out of the situation was some kind of murder-suicide pact feels a little thin to me."

"That's why it would work. We wouldn't be expecting it. It gives them the element of surprise!"

"Yyy, we had the element of surprise. We dropped out of the sky on them. The element of surprise is great, but it requires a certain amount of follow-through. Killing your own population to take out your opposition, that's madness. Nobody wins because everybody's dead."

I'd boxed him in with reason and Yyy found this very frustrating. He turned and started to crawl away from the controls.

"The reason you don't like my idea is because you didn't think of it first," he said as he disappeared behind the bulkhead.

Which was the last time I saw him alive.

•

"I don't think Yyy is breathing any more."

It was our third night of plodding through the red hills of Earth when Ppp came to the command sling and, very apologetically it seemed to me, brought the news that Yyy was dead.

Yyy was in his hammock, gently swinging with the motion of the tripod risers. He was silent. All the noises and wheezing and expectoration had left him. There was a little slimy trail of something from the corner of his mouth dripping to form a small, dark, circular stain on the hammock mat. His eyes were half closed. I closed them the rest of the way.

"What's happening to us?" Ppp asked from the edge of the bulkhead.

"I don't know. Get the scroll."

We stopped the tripod where we were, lowered the cabin to the ground, and wrestled Yyy's body through the hatch. We carried him some distance from the tripod and set him down where the red creeper was deep. It settled around him, attracted to the fading warmth of his body.

Ppp dipped the tip of his dominant tentacle into the flask of distillate and drew a moist line down the center of Yyy's face, from crown to lips, then another, intersecting line across his closed eyes. Sectioning his face into quarters.

We touched off the distillate with the miniature convector. A cross of pale blue flame bloomed on Yyy's face and quickly spread to cover him completely. There was little smoke.

"Go ahead," I said to Ppp.

He looked at me. "Go ahead?"

"Read something from the scrolls."

"I thought, maybe, you'd want to do it," he said. "I mean, you're in charge."

I wanted to tell him how much I wasn't in charge. How much I was coming around to the conclusion that nobody was in charge of anything.

"All right," I said and put my tentacle out. Ppp gave me the scroll.

I was going to pick something from the beginning and get it over with, but reading it, looking at all that mumbo jumbo about greatness and honor and destiny, I couldn't do it. I rolled up the scroll and looked at Yyy being consumed by the blue fire that was waiting for all of us.

"Typee," I said. "Piazzatalls, Typee, Typee."

Ppp looked very confused.

"Ah, is that from the scrolls?"

"No."

"Aren't you supposed to say something from the scrolls?"

"I'm starting a new tradition," I told him, then tried to remember the rest of what was on the first leaf of the folder back in the wrecked shelter.

"Hurmahn Me Lvell. Omoo, Omoo, Typee."

I could see Ppp out of the corner of my eye, looking down at the blue flames moving in waves all over Yyy.

"Deeeahx Ahward. EeecccIii Broohwehey."

Ppp assumed what I was saying was in some way appropriate. It must have sounded right to him. What difference does it make what you say over somebody who's dead?

"Load-don: Camm Pspun Loy Soy ack coh."

Poor Yyy, folding in on himself, turning to ash in front of us. His eyes and beak and mouth pulling together as they burned. His face getting smaller and smaller, and puckering up. Like he was about to start whistling.

"Poor Yyy," I said. "Poor, poor Yyy."

The next sound I made surprised me as much as it did Ppp. I felt myself tremble and I looked up at the moon and the misty ring that hung around it and I howled.

"Typee! Omoo! Etc! Etc! Etc!"

And then we were quiet as we watched Yyy burn.

•

In the morning we scattered the ashes and started back along the beacon to Mmm's camp. I took the tripod off auto-stabilize so I could request more speed with the manual override. I didn't want to spend another night out here on our own. Whatever was going to happen to Ppp and me, I didn't want us to be alone when it happened.

Ppp was behind and to one side of me in the cabin. Neither one of us said much for most of the morning.

Then Ppp said, "Something's wrong with the creeper."

I'd wondered when he was going to notice.

The creeper wasn't as red as it was a day ago. It was darker. And it was picking up some kind of gray in the high places.

The farther we went, the more the creeper changed. The more gray it became as it climbed down the hills and along the valleys, breaking up on the water and starting to flow downstream.

And this was happening faster and faster as we went on our way. We stopped talking and could almost see the red creeper dying in front of us.

•

A couple of hours later, Ppp pointed at something down in the valley we'd entered.

"Look."

What he saw was one of Mmm's tripods standing sentry over the camp. It was beautiful seeing that machine drawn up to its full height, watching over the cylinder and the camp.

I pushed the throttle and we were galloping toward Mmm and his crew. A couple of minutes and we'd . . .

"Vvv, what's that?"

Ppp was pointing his tentacle at an amorphous cloud of something black that was circling the cabin of the sentry tripod. Something like smoke, that didn't move like smoke.

I slowed the tripod, but we kept going. When we got closer what had looked like smoke from a distance reconciled into a swarm of small black animals swimming in the air around the cabin. Animals with wings growing out of their backs. A billowing of black specks all around the cabin, and landing on it.

I saw the blood before Ppp did. I stopped our tripod close

enough to the sentry to see the length of tentacle hanging from the side hatch. What was left of a tentacle.

The flying animals were swooping in, one after another, to peck bits of flesh from the appendage. Others were flying through the hatch and coming out with bleeding prizes in their beaks and claws.

Ppp moaned at my side. He had turned to look down at the camp. There were the corpses of seven or eight Martians on the ground, one hanging from the lip of the cylinder. Nothing moved except for the black wings all around them.

I couldn't believe how much I'd counted on the camp still being there. I thought there was a good chance I would never move from the spot where I sat. Then Ppp brushed past me and grabbed the weapons control. He turned the oculus toward the sentry tripod and discharged the convector.

The sets of wings turned into points of fire falling, trailing wisps of gray smoke. Some moved after hitting the ground. Most did not.

Then Ppp focused the convector on the cowl and cabin of the sentry tripod. It was instantly covered with ripples of boiling air. There was a flash and a muffled explosion from inside the cabin as the interior started to burn.

Ppp almost knocked me from my sling when he swung the convector around and aimed it at the camp and the cylinder. The bodies caught fire. In a moment flames were lurching out of the open cylinder, roaring like the mouth of a forge.

Ppp shut off the convector and sat at the back of the cabin. We watched the fires, and then I heard Ppp whispering behind me. At first I didn't recognize what he was saying. Then I figured it out.

"Typee, Typee," he said. "Piazzatalls, Typee, Typee. Hurmahn Me Lvell. Omoo, Omoo, Typee. Typee! Omoo! Etc! Etc! Etc!"

•

We watched the fires burn themselves out. It was dark then and we crawled back to our hammocks. I felt one or both of us wouldn't wake up in the morning. But we both did, and Ppp was clearly as surprised as I was.

We crawled into the cabin and looked out at what was left of the camp and the sentry tripod.

Ppp turned to me and said, "I think the invasion is over."

I was going to tell him I agreed, but there didn't seem to be any real need for speaking. Anything I said would have been more words, and I didn't see the need for them. Besides, it hurt my throat to talk.

I nodded my head.

We looked out at the countryside for a very long time. Then Ppp turned to me again.

"Where should we go now?" he asked.

"Where would you like to go?"

Ppp gave this question a considerable amount of thought, which I appreciated, since I certainly didn't want the choice to fall to me.

"I don't know," he finally said. "Maybe someplace high. A hill."

"Why a hill?"

"I guess, so we can see all around us. So we'll know where we are."

This seemed as reasonable to me as anything else would

that day. I turned the cabin on its turret and we started walking.

•

Everywhere we walked the creeper was dying and the ground was going from red to gray right in front of us. The wind would pick up the dust of the dead creeper and spin it through the air and pile it up in dunes in the nooks and low places. It was happening very quickly all around us.

My head, my whole body was pounding and sloshing. What air I could get into my lungs felt like it was being drawn through a wet sponge.

We went on for a long time, looking for the best possible hill to die on.

"They'll never know what happened. Back home. Will they?"

Ppp wasn't looking at me when he asked this, he was looking ahead through the quartz at the color draining from the countryside.

"They'll tell them something," I assured him. "Not what really happened, but they'll have to come up with something. They can't afford to look bad, so you can figure they'll make us all look like a bunch of martyrs and heroes."

"Heroes?"

"Heroes."

"Wow. Yyy would have liked that."

"Yes, he would have been very happy about that."

And then Ppp cleared his throat as best he could and said to me, "It's been an honor to serve with you, Vvv."

I turned to look at him. He meant it. He meant it with a sincerity that cut through me and made me feel like the lowest Martian imaginable.

"The honor, Ppp, has been all mine," I told him.

I was surprised by the smile I felt stretching my face in reaction to the ludicrous formality of what we were saying. But it made me feel better, responding the way I did. Ceremony is the last bit of civilization to go. It's the thing that gives us an ending instead of, I don't know, just stopping.

It was night when we found our hill.

It looked down into a steeply cut valley with a narrow river twisting through it. The moon was bright overhead and that cut deep shadows through the cardo nest that hugged the near bank of the river. The water was quickly clearing itself of dead creeper and the moon made it a shifting silver thread. There were no lights from the nest that had one of those tall, pointy structures all the big nests seem to have. Looking in the opposite direction from the top of the hill, we could see all the way to a great glistening expanse resting against the edge of the land. It was the ocean we'd seen with Hhh and the others. However long ago that was.

"What about here?" I asked Ppp.

"Oh, this'll be fine. Don't you think so?"

I looked at the moon. No longer full, but the roundness of the thing was still defined. The parts in shadow blocked out a crescent of stars behind it.

I stopped the tripod and banked the motors.

We stayed in the cabin and looked at the moon.

I felt like the inside of my skin was burning. That any moment it was going to set and crack like fired clay and all my insides would spill out into a steaming pile on the deck of the tripod.

I didn't think the cardos were poisoning themselves to get to us, but something was killing us. Killing us faster than the Leadership could replace us. Not as if that was something they were interested in doing. No, no profit in that. Time to cut their losses and declare victory.

I hope Mmm was able to get a message back to Mars about Qqq being the first Martian to touch the surface of the Earth, I really do. I sincerely hope they put up a statue in his honor. A big one. Centrally located near a major transportation hub in an area with first-rate accommodations for all the pilgrims who'll come every year for the big celebrations, the pageants and festivals and commemorations. Seriously, I hope they do.

I hope they immediately inaugurate a memorial subscription fund. One with reasonable overhead allowances in order to attract the best minds to the project.

If they don't do it right, it might give the impression all this was a big waste of time and we died so far from home for no good reason.

Can't have that.

The moon was getting bigger. The bright crescent was expanding, taking up more of the surface until it was full again and drifting closer to the Earth. And there was another moon beside it, the same size. Then a third moon. And something slung underneath the three moons on tethers and nets.

I'd never seen anything like it, but I'd had it described to me. It was one of the ships Ppp saw in his dream. The ones that drifted off the Plain of Barso and left him on Mars. Beautiful tapered silver ships with a needle at the nose and swept-back fins that made them look like they were going incredibly fast even when they were motionless.

"Hey, Ppp!" I shouted as I pulled myself around to look back at him. "Your ship is here. They came back for you!"

Ppp didn't move. He was silent, slumped down on the floor. He was holding the flask of distillate in one tentacle and had dipped the tip of his dominant tentacle into the liquid. Then he drew one line straight down the center of his face from crown to lips and another line across his closed eyes. Sectioning his face into quarters.

When I looked back at the sky, Ppp's ship had vanished.

•

In the morning I didn't have the strength to get Ppp out of the tripod. Frankly, I didn't see much point to it, given the nature of the situation. So I arranged him in his hammock, then defeated the bypass on the convectors and set the tripod on the ground so I could get out. Then I sealed the tripod and sent it up to its full height.

I backed away as the convectors started to overheat and smoke crawled out from under the cowling, coiling up over the tripod to where it was pulled across the sky by the breeze.

Flames appeared behind the quartz.

It was the best I felt I could do under the circumstances,

and I was reasonably sure Ppp would understand and appreciate the effort.

I moved back, down the hill, looked up at the burning tripod and shouted a salute.

"Ulla!" I called.

And my salute was oddly answered by a sound from the nest down in the valley. A loud, metallic bong, deep and full of resonance, called up the slope to me. It came, I reasoned, from the tall pointy tower. Like the one we'd knocked over on our way to the sea with Hhh.

The sound seemed to cling to the end of my call.

Ulllllaoong.

I settled myself in the granular remains of the red creeper and looked down the hill to the nest by the river still in shadow. The sun edged over the far side of the valley, and the light from it moved down the gray remains of the creeper hugging the hill beneath me. When the sun got high enough and the blanket of light extended far enough down the hill, I saw a single figure in white walking toward me.

It was upright and not suffering from the excesses of gravity so I assumed it was an Earth cardo.

Poor Ppp, I thought. Here comes this cardo walking up the hill to sit with me and discuss matters and settle all our differences and reach a glorious transplanetary concordance and Ppp was going to miss out on all of that because of being dead.

It was an Earth cardo, dressed in white, and the closer it got, the more familiar it seemed to me. A single wrap of white fabric around its lower appendages, more white fitted around the torso, transparent white fabric like a halo behind its head. White sacks of fabric around its upper pseudos, and holding a circular collection of vegetable matter as it walked toward me.

How's that for an epic coincidence? Or is it irony, Mmm? Coming up the hill toward me was the cardo who was rendered in the image I found pushed into the case with the golden gears back where we crashed.

The cardo in white continued up the hill toward me. I was trying to remember how long ago it had been since I saw the image when I realized the figure approaching me was changing as it got closer to me.

Her hair was shifting color and her eyes were getting larger. The eyes were changing color, too. They were becoming golden, like her hair. And then I noticed the fabric around her was shifting, rearranging itself across her body.

Her body?

Her?

The fabric loosened and unfurled and fell straight from her shoulders to the ground. The breeze pressed the fabric against her body and you could see this cardo wasn't a stick, but had a softness to her. And she wasn't a cardo anymore.

The sun climbed above the crest of the far hill and found the female and traced her with so much light.

She was one of the old Martians. The ancients. Dark they were, and golden-eyed. The old one from Ppp's dream. I knew it had to be the same. Somewhere along the way, Ppp had slipped his dream into my mind and here it was. Here she was. A gift from Ppp.

She stopped in front of me. Not too close, not too far away. She wanted me to be able to see all of her. It wasn't the face of a cardo, but you could see where the features of a cardo might have come from in her face. Her beautiful face. Soft and kind.

She smiled. Smiling lifted her cheeks. There was a topography to her face, plains and curves and elevations, and those beautiful golden eyes.

"Hello, Vvv," she said to me.

"Hello," I said to her.

I was looking at her so intensely I hadn't noticed how intensely she was studying me. As if she was trying to imagine how I ended up looking the way I did.

She sighed. Then she said, "My name is Ylla."

"Were you named after the mountains on Mars?"

"No," she said. "The mountains were named after me. I came first. They named the mountains later. They thought I was mythological. But I'm not. I mean, I am now, but I wasn't then."

"I don't understand."

"I don't know if understanding will make much difference at this point, Vvv, but I thought I should try to explain."

I couldn't think of anything to say except, "Enthusiasm makes the difference."

"It can certainly make matters worse, that's for sure," she said and gently shook her head. "There you sit, not much more than a brain in a ball of flesh. Simultaneously pathetic and repulsive, with those fleshy, ropey limbs dangling down, squirming about. That's what enthusiasm has done to you."

"Ppp saw you in a dream."

"I know. He was sweet. I tried to explain to him. At least show it to him."

"Ppp's dead."

She looked up, over me, to the burning tripod at the crest of the hill.

"I know," she said.

"They're all dead."

She looked at me. I think she wanted to look at me with love, but she found I was too ugly for that gesture. The best she could come up with was pity.

"Almost all," she said. "You'll be one of the last to go."

Then Ylla gathered the front of the white fabric she wore and kneeled on the ground in front of me. She tilted her head a few degrees to the right.

"I want you to know how sorry we all are about how it worked out," she said in such a musical whisper of a voice. A voice like crystals humming.

"You mean with the invasion?" I asked.

"Well, the invasion, of course, but mostly everything leading up to the invasion. Honestly, we never thought it would come to this. I want to assure you, we had nothing but the best intentions."

Her breath was cool and sweet on my face.

"And it happened all so long ago," she told me.

"What did?"

"The Migration. The Pilgrimage. The Nomadization. So many names for the same desire: To bring the gift of Martian culture, Martian progress, Martian life to other, less fortunate worlds."

I had no idea what she was talking about.

She reached out with her slender upper appendages and held my head with her hands. Her touch was cool against my burning skin.

Her hands.

Hands.

She looked at me with her impossible golden eyes and spoke.

"We danced and sang by the canals and spun light in the air and thought, 'Why shouldn't the entire solar system be as perfect as we?' 'Why stop with the solar system?' someone said. 'Why not the universe?' So a billion years ago, some of us said goodbye to all we loved and sailed off to set the universe right. And we were remarkably successful at it. The cosmos teems with life because of Mars. That's something you should be proud of. Really. Unfortunately, the farther we went, the farther we wanted to go. And back home . . . "

She stood and opened her arms, the fabric of her gown falling straight from neck to hem, with all the beauty and drama of a column. A column of . . . I heard a word in my head I didn't know. Alabaster.

She reached out to my upturned face.

"Back home this was happening to you."

"What was happening?" I begged her.

"You evolved. That evolution was accelerated and guided by the geniuses and societal fabricators who stayed behind.

Drab, practical minds who didn't want to come with us and live between the stars. Truth be told, I think they resented our leaving. Now you are what you are. Unrecognizable to me as Martian."

She shook her head slightly.

"Oh, Vvv, we were so beautiful," she said, her golden hair moving behind her, touching her shoulders as it absorbed the sunlight. "The way I look to you right now? That's nothing. That's being filtered because my beauty is completely staggering. I am what Martians once looked like."

As if Ylla had willed it, soft wind swept down the hillside and pressed her gown against her body. That shape, it was the grace all cardos have been falling from ever since creation.

She saw my eyes tracing her shape under her gown. Ylla furrowed her brow and did something with her lips, pressing them together.

"Poor, poor Vvv. Ultimately, in the name of perfection, those left in charge eliminated sex. What a terrible shame," she sighed. "Of course, being geniuses and societal fabricators they probably didn't know what they were missing. Having erased our 'imperfections,' it was imperative that they erase all evidence of our existence. They turned us into ghosts and legends. Vanished gods. But legends are what last and ghosts know all the best stories. As for gods, well, gods never completely go away. Do they?"

I managed to push one word from my lips: "Why?"

"Why did we leave?" she asked. I nodded as best I could.

She sighed and looked toward the ocean in the distance. "I suppose it was something we couldn't help. After all, we were descended from Orovars, a seafaring race. They explored the oceans of Mars, conquering and claiming what they found. Then the seas dried up and there's nothing left of that heritage except pleasure sailing on the canals. I'm sometimes troubled by the gnawing suspicion we may have been terribly overcompensating for something."

She stood there, the breeze pressing against her from the front, the morning sun pressing against her from the back. It made me mad. Angry about decisions made millions of years before I was created. I couldn't have stopped it. Couldn't have stopped it anymore than I could have kept the cylinder from crushing that cardo. But that didn't make me less angry.

Ylla saw the anger behind the pain in my eyes. She put her open hands beside her face and made a small O of her mouth. I got the impression this was some stylized gesture that meant something in her time, but was unintelligible to me. She lowered her arms, looked at the ground, then looked at me.

"Much as I don't want to hurt your feelings, Vvv, it is my sad duty to inform you that, as a result of generation after generation of genetic mischief, you represent an evolutionary cul-de-sac. The Mars you left behind will continue its stuttering decline and collapse over the next thousand years or so until there's nothing left."

"Nothing?"

"Well, a few million years from now maybe there'll be something left in the sand that'll get another chance. Who knows? It might work out better next time. At least until the sun dies and swallows the inner planets."

"Did the cardos poison us?" It was getting so painful to speak.

"Not as such," Ylla said. "You're dying because you're here, but it's not something they're doing on purpose. I suppose you could pin that on evolution, too. If you wanted to."

I was trying to understand what she was saying, but the fever that was searing my brain made it hard to concentrate. She saw that on my face and felt sorry for me. Somebody feeling sorry for Vvv. That's a first. And, I guess, a last.

"Believe me," she pleaded. "We never thought it would end like this. I'm afraid we didn't think it all the way through. It seemed like such a good idea at the time and something took hold of us."

"En-thus-i-asim." It burned my throat to say the word.

"Once you let it loose it's hard to control."

There was the groan of metal and the splintering of quartz. Ylla looked past me. I turned around as much as I could and watched the burning cabin of the tripod lurch and fall and tumble past us down the hill, trailing smoke and flame and leaving the risers stuck in the ground, supporting nothing. Ylla watched the lopsided remains of the tripod cabin roll to a stop halfway between us and the nest by the river.

"We wanted more," she said as she looked at the crushed

tripod. "We were afraid of dying and couldn't see why we should be made to do so. We wanted to live forever. So we bred our way across the sky."

When Ylla turned back to me her golden eyes shimmered with tears.

"Please understand, Vvv. You see, we knew we were beautiful and thought, therefore, we were wise."

Ylla closed her golden eyes and stretched out her arms and put her cool hands on my face. And then she sang to me.

It was a sobbing alternation of two notes, "Ulla, ulla, ulla, ulla." Not a shout, not a cry, but something smooth like the calm water of Tirra Canal, sighing past the bow of your skimmer.

I opened my parched lips and tried to sing with her. I don't know if anything came out of me besides my sour breath.

"Ulla, ulla, ulla, ulla…"

There were other sounds now in the valley. Other deep ringing sounds from other towers in other nests. Bottomless, solemn sounds like ancient crystals vibrating on the sides of mountains when the sun hits them and heats the air. When the rocks tremble and spread the light everywhere. I closed my eyes.

We sang with the bells. The bells sang with us. Ylla and

me.

Bells?

"Ulla, ulla, ulla, ulla…"

Her voice faded into the sound of the bells until I couldn't hear her anymore and the coolness of her hands faded from my face. I listened to the bells, then I opened my eyes and looked down along the hill toward the nest.

I saw figures on the hill, moving up the hill, moving toward me. Earth cardos. A great many of them. Moving very fast, clambering up the hill to get to me. They're shouting something. Many of them have long sticks and rods. They hold them in the air. Swinging them in the air.

None of these sticks or rods have white rags tied to their ends.

I closed my eyes and tried to concentrate on the sound of the bells.
If I'm lucky, I'll die before they reach me.

These creatures coming up the hill.

These children.

The children of Mars.

—AN AFTERWORD—

I have encountered much skepticism about the authenticity of this narrative. There has been criticism and occasionally outright derision of my claims. I suppose concern for one's reputation demands a response. But, frankly, after what we've all been through, the thought of worrying about such things as reputation seems petty if not absurd. So, this is not a defense, but a simple statement of how this manuscript came into being.

For many years I was a reporter for a newspaper in New York City. I was not very good at it. I wasn't able to generate much interest in the sort of stories I was expected to write and was more fascinated by things that were of no interest to my employers. I was, for example, more intrigued by how the married couple who owned and operated a basement café for more than twenty-five years managed to do so without ever speaking to each other, than I was interested in the ax murder that occurred on the rooftop of the building housing the café.

There was considerable talk about my being fired. This talk commenced about a week after I was hired. But I had a benefactor at the paper: The wife of the publisher, who was riding in the carriage that knocked me down in the middle of Broadway one spring morning. She insisted that her husband hire me on his paper and that my position would be secure however long I wanted it.

The editors tolerated me and offered me certain obtuse assignments that were not part of any conventional newsbeat. I remained and was, to the best of my ability, harmless and entertaining and occasionally resourceful. And that is the path that led me to the account you've now read.

In the last years of the nineteenth century, I made the acquaintance of Mr. Arthur Bosco of the Vinegar Hill section of Brooklyn. Without putting too fine a point on it, I thought Mr. Bosco was a charlatan when I met him.

I had been given a letter by my editor sent to us from a young woman who was writing out of desperation to see if our newspaper could help her where the authorities seemed powerless. Her mother was seeing a so-called medium who was helping the young lady's mother "communicate with the dead." Apparently, the woman's mother, a Mrs. A, had reached that point in life when death begins to accumulate around us. This woman had experienced more loss than she could withstand; her husband, two children including a baby stillborn, her parents, and three siblings.

I arranged for the letter writer, Miss A, to meet me at our offices on Chatham Street. She was a modest, attractive, and impressively levelheaded young lady. Her concern was very real. While Mr. Bosco, the purported medium, had not as yet asked for any money, she was certain it was merely a matter of time before he revealed his criminal intentions. The police told her there was nothing they could do until an actual crime had been committed. She dared not wait, for fear of how this miscreant's falsehoods could affect her mother.

We discussed a ploy in which I would be able to meet Mr. Bosco and make an assessment of his claims and objectives. Miss A would tell her mother she had met a young man at work who was very interested in the supernatural and would like to meet Mr. Bosco. Would it be possible for this acquaintance to accompany Mrs. A when she next traveled to Brooklyn?

The young lady reported back to me that Mrs. A would be more than happy to have her daughter's friend attend a séance. She hoped this would lead to the daughter's deeper involvement in the spirit world.

I had been to séances before while

researching an article on fake spiritualists. I assumed that's why the editor selected me for this assignment. Séances all tend to be the same incense-clouded flummery, the same hoary histrionics to which cling the unpleasant odor of traveling carnivals. That plus the cruel promise of peace and contact and heavenly assurance, purchasable on a sliding scale adjusted to the wealth of the client. I was expecting something similar as I followed Miss A and her mother up the stairs to Mr. Bosco's third-floor apartment. But I was surprised. The first of several surprises that day and subsequently.

The door was opened by a cherubic woman whose smile might have been the result of how tightly her vermilion hair was pulled back into a bun. Mrs. A introduced me to Mrs. Bosco and we entered the apartment.

Mrs. Bosco led us along a narrow hallway with doors on either side. Most were shut, but one door was open and through it I glimpsed a kitchen where a girl of perhaps thirteen was slicing potatoes.

The hallway took us to a parlor set in one of the rounded corners of the building. The room was dim. Heavy drapes were closed at all the windows. A large, heavy, round, mahogany dining table occupied the center of this round room. At the center of the round table was a round silver serving tray on which sat a clear glass beaker sixteen inches or so in height. There was an amber liquid in the beaker and, suspended from a porcelain lid, two strips of metal were immersed in the fluid. The metal strips were enveloped in a sheen of minute bubbles that continually effervesced toward the top of the beaker.

Somehow this apparatus was producing a soft glow that touched the room with a light suggestive of great age. As if it had traveled some impossible distance to arrive at this glass prison. I was impressed with what I then thought of as the subtle stagecraft of the setting. Whatever this was, it was no run-of-the-mill carnie ploy.

Mrs. Bosco went to fetch her husband, leaving the two ladies and myself alone in the parlor. There was a whispering in the room, something like the stroking on a single string on a double bass. The sound was everywhere, but seemed to be emanating from the glass beaker. I leaned over the table to get a better look at the thing. Two coiled wires were attached to contacts on the lid. I assumed, correctly, that these were attached to the two metal plates suspended in the solution. The coiled wires led to the edge of the table, where they terminated in two leather straps, one larger than the other. I was about to pick up one of the straps when I was stopped by a man's voice.

"I would advise against that." The voice

was not urgent. It was not a command, not really a warning, it was a dispassionate statement of something it would be wise of me to avoid.

I turned and saw the man I took to be Mr. Bosco standing in the doorway, the hallway extending to its vanishing point behind him. He was perhaps fifty, tall, a great wave of white hair above a face cut deeply by sun and time.

"Dear Mr. Bosco," Mrs. A began. "This is my daughter's friend Mr. Dougherty. The gentleman you were kind enough to invite."

We exchanged greetings and shook hands. He invited us to sit. We did. Bosco, as I anticipated, sat at the place nearest the two wires.

Bosco looked at me, his eyes measuring me from somewhere back behind his prodigious brows.

"I know why Mrs. A is here, and I know why Miss A has come. But why, sir, are you so interested in my work?"

I told him I was deeply curious about all things having to do with spiritualism.

"Then I'm afraid you'll be very disappointed," Bosco said. "What goes on here isn't spiritualism, it is science."

"But I understood that you've put Mrs. A in contact with members of her family who have . . . passed on?" I offered.

"Died. There is no kindness in euphemisms, young man."

"You have a scientific means of communicating with the dead?"

"The dead are with us, Mr. Dougherty. Above us."

With which he pointed upwards.

"You mean in Heaven?" I asked.

"No, I mean above us. The air we are breathing takes up but one level of a multilayered envelope. As mountain climbers have long understood, the higher you go the thinner the air. But what is above the air we breathe? What keeps it from escaping into the vacuum of space? I have read the works of Gustave Hermite, Teisserenc de Bort in France, Assmann in Germany."

Mr. Bosco cupped his hands as if to cradle an imaginary ball.

"Layers, Mr. Dougherty. Spheres of differing elemental makeup set inside each other. Different temperatures, different barometric pressure, different purposes and properties. Discreet, but permeable. All held together, balanced. There is the Troposphere, the Stratosphere, and, as I have discovered and named, the Thanasphere."

"Thanasphere?"

"Thanasphere, Mr. Dougherty. A layer of the Earth's atmosphere above the rest that contains a unique psychic-electrical force. It is this outer sphere that shelters all the others. We continue to breathe here on

Earth because of the Thanasphere."

"And what does the Thanasphere consist of?" I asked him.

"Souls, Mr. Dougherty," he said, leaning slightly forward for emphasis. "Human souls. The Thanasphere is, simply stated, the region of the dead. It is there the surviving individual personalities and memories of the absent are stitched together to contain and protect the very air we breathe. Our lives are their gift to us. They are the aggregate of all that has gone before. The immortal purpose that awaits each one of us."

This might seem laughable to you, reading this description of the Thanasphere, but it was a very different thing hearing Mr. Bosco's confident voice weaving the threads of his theory in that dim room.

He elaborated: When connected to precise points on Mr. Bosco's body by special rare-earth wires, the magnetic plates suspended in the beaker filled with a particular galvanic fluid had permitted him to listen to the voices of the dead above us, and, following chemical and electrical refinements, to actually engage in conversations with individual members of that departed society.

I understood the concern Miss A held for her mother, but at the same time there was something difficult to resist in Mr.

Bosco's presentation.

Perhaps it was the warmth of the day, compounded by the closed drapes, that allowed his voice to find a way, at least momentarily, around my intellectual defenses. I have since learned how close healthy skepticism is to blind cynicism.

We sat around the table, Mr. Bosco close to the coiled wires, Mrs. A to his right, Miss A to his left, and myself across the table from him. Mrs. Bosco arrived to close the door to the parlor. I could hear her footsteps diminishing in the hall as Mr. Bosco secured one of the wire-connected straps to his left wrist and used the other, longer strap to encircle his head.

Bosco did not ask us to hold hands or concentrate or any of the other stage business I'd come to expect from spiritualists. Instead he rested his palms on the tabletop and closed his eyes.

Soon I felt the room fill with an unnatural stillness. As if the very molecules of the air were slowing and rearranging themselves. The flow of miniature bubbles crawling along the sides of the metal strips increased. The beaker glowed brighter and the level of light in the room increased. But this latter effect was not the result of the beaker acting as some sort of lamp. It was the air itself that seemed to contain the light.

The sound I detected when we first entered the room became more pronounced. It was part of the air as much as the sourceless illumination that filled the space around the table and the people sitting there. A low sound, at the bottom edge of hearing, almost more vibration than sound.

Bosco opened his eyes and turned to Mrs. A.

"Mrs. A," he whispered. "Does this have any meaning for you?"

With which, Mr. Bosco puckered his lips and whistled a tune from my childhood. The words came to me in the remembered voice of Millicent, who cared for me from infancy till her death when I was ten years old.

Cherry ripe, cherry ripe,
Ripe I cry,
Full and fair ones
Come and buy . . .

Mrs. A listened, then shook her head. The tune had no meaning for her. Mr. Bosco then looked at Miss A and saw no sign of recognition on her face. Then Bosco looked across the table to me, and waited. As he waited, he whistled.

Cherry ripe, cherry ripe,

Ripe I cry,
Full and fair ones
Come and buy . . .

Mr. Bosco closed his eyes again. He listened for a moment, then opened his eyes and looked at me.

"The young lady understands if Gerry doesn't remember; she knew him so long ago."

A nursery song, a childhood version of my middle name used to avoid confusion with my father. Certainly these things might have been discoverable. They might have been, but . . . From this turmoil of mind I heard myself speak:

"Yes, Millicent. I remember you." And then I asked: "Are you all right?"

Mr. Bosco turned his head as if to listen. Then his features flinched and contorted, as if he'd suddenly been seized by a vicious toothache. He grasped the edge of the table and closed his eyes, squeezing them shut until they disappeared behind horizontals of wrinkled flesh.

The light in the air around us hesitated.

Mr. Bosco opened his eyes. He looked around the room and seemed surprised by his surroundings. Then he spoke, but not in the voice we'd heard from him up until then. His calm, soothing tenor had become something submerged and mucilaginous. If mud had a voice I imagine it would sound like this.

I assumed the sounds to be the equivalent of words or parts of words, but they had no meaning to the listeners in the room. They were a string of moist noises split by sibilant hisses. There was nothing recognizable in what he was saying, but there was the unmistakable sense that the utterances were powered by fear and pain.

Bosco spoke like this for perhaps half a minute, ending in a rising crescendo repeating one group of sounds that formed what might have been a single word, uttered over and over and over, as a drowning man might invoke a deity's intervention before being pulled beneath the waves. One word, repeated perhaps a dozen times before Bosco groped at the straps around his wrist and head and tore them away, breaking contact with the beaker and its contents.

Light withdrew from the air. The room was dark except for a thin vertical of sunlight at the gap between two of the drapes.

Mrs. Bosco burst into the room and went to her husband. The girl who had been slicing potatoes in the kitchen came as far as the doorway, but did not cross the threshold.

Bosco grabbed for his wife's hand and pulled his face against her bosom, oblivious to the other people in the room. Aside from Mrs. Bosco stroking the back of her husband's head, we were all motionless. Like a tableau vivant at the end of a disturbing and indecipherable play.

A minute, perhaps longer, and Bosco turned to face his guests.

"Inexplicable," he said. "Most inexplicable. I've never . . . Unprecedented interaction. An incursion of some sort. Yes, an incursion from . . . somewhere. I don't have an explanation for . . . I'm afraid . . . Yes, you'll all have to excuse me."

Mr. Bosco continued to apologize as his wife helped him from his chair and out of the parlor. He promised he would make the necessary adjustments to his device before Mrs. A's next appointment and was muttering something about "unfavorable atmospheric conditions" as he and his wife stepped into a room along the hallway and closed the door after them. We were let out of the apartment by the girl who had been slicing the potatoes. I learned much later that this was Mr. Bosco's niece. We took the stairs to the street where Mrs. A waited in her carriage while I walked a few yards away with her daughter for a quick conversation about the séance.

I admitted to being flummoxed by the afternoon; if Bosco was a confidence artist, he was a very odd one. I found myself coming to the conclusion that Bosco was sincere in his fantastic beliefs. If Mrs. A found solace in these shenanigans, and Bosco did not reveal any criminal motive behind his mumming and conjuring, it might be best to leave well enough alone. I asked Miss A to contact me if there were any developments in the situation. In the meanwhile I would do some checking on my own into Bosco and his origins.

Fortunately, she did not ask me who Millicent was.

Miss A joined her mother in their carriage and I watched them ride away. I have not seen them since. I hope they are still alive.

I returned to the newspaper office where the Associated Press wire was carrying the first dispatches about what was unfolding in England. Over the next twenty-four hours there were similar reports of projectiles falling from the skies around the world and disgorging creatures begging description. These were followed by tales of hellish weapons, massive destruction, and wholesale slaughter. It was during the second night that a cylinder fell close to New York City, near the town of Grovers Mill, New Jersey.

In the chaos and horror of the days that followed, the machinations of a penny-ante Brooklyn confidence man lost what little import they might ever have had.

For we found ourselves participating in the rout of civilization.

If you were fortunate enough to live in some corner of the world that escaped unscathed from the Martian assault, there is little point in my trying to describe what life was like under the heel of the tripods. For the rest of us it was a rapidly enlarging spiral of death, suffering, loss, bravery, cowardice, and, perhaps worst of all, the sense of being abandoned, by God, if you were so inclined, or by reason itself.

And then the mayhem stopped. The terrible engines of destruction froze where they stood, as if transfixed by some gorgon more horrible than themselves. The grotesque invaders were all dead.

There followed songs of victory and tales of a vanquished enemy. But, really, this was no victory. There had been no war. A war requires two sides of approximately equal strength and intent. What we faced wasn't an opposing army, but an implacable evil, exhibiting no more concern for the human race than do the forces of nature itself. The same invisible nature that eventually smote our adversaries with Biblical swiftness.

Around the world and in various

ways, groups of people had been able to incapacitate a few dozen tripods and dispatch their crews. But no battles were waged, no campaigns executed, no alliances forged. No, the singular thing those days had in common with war was the tremendous amount of blood involved.

The bleeding had stopped on both sides, but there was nothing you could call peace. We were left with a scratchy form of anxiety that still hangs in the air like static electricity.

Few speak of it, but most of us understand there is every possibility that we are experiencing a mere pause before our ultimate quietus. Yet we proceed, if not progress, momentarily obliged to live with this uneasy salvation.

We walk around the city, a city intent on rebuilding itself as if replacing buildings could make us forget the thousands crushed when the original structures fell, constantly tending to a strained and artificial normality. On your walk you might catch some of your fellow citizens occasionally looking back over their shoulders, not at who might be following them on the street, but looking up, at the sky, which will never again be without the threat of death.

The sky has become an open wound through which horror could pour at any instant. The blue enameled dome of day and the

star-spattered night have ceased to be
sources of poetic inspiration and become,
instead, inescapable reminders of our naked
vulnerability.

The city will never return to what it
was. Life itself has changed.

•

Our visitors left behind numerous souvenirs.
Dead Martians float in jars of preservatives
at many museums while scientists and
engineers pick over their machines.

The examples of Martian machinery
recovered in the New York area are treated
as anthropological artifacts and have been
kept at the American Museum of Natural
History. There among the mummies and fossils
are held the gleaming metal and quartz
creations of that distant and malevolent
race. Examination of the mechanical objects
progressed slowly and with much caution
following the disasters at the Ealing and
South Kensington laboratories in London.

It was more than a year after the invasion
that I along with several other reporters
were invited to the museum to witness a
demonstration of one of the undamaged spool
devices found in a fallen tripod. Dr. E.
J. Prescott and his associate Mr. Phillip
W. Sloan of the Rensselaer Polytechnic
Institute in Troy, New York, had been

able to activate what they discovered was a machine for mechanically recording and reproducing the sounds of Martian speech. We in the press would be the first beyond a small coterie of scientists and public officials to hear the voice and language of the Martians.

The event took place in a small lecture hall at the museum. The press was first invited to come to the stage for a close look at the device, but under no circumstances should we attempt to touch it. The machine rested on a table. It was perhaps two feet long, essentially tubular in shape, made of the clear quartz the Martians used for glass and a polished black substance which appeared to me to be metal. The quartz and metal were joined in some way, but it was impossible to detect any seam at the joining place. Under the quartz we could see a band of flexible metal held between rollers.

After walking around the object, behaving like a tribe of natives on some South Sea isle gathered around a small printing press washed up from a wreck and trying to reason out its origin and purpose, we took our seats. Dr. Prescott and Mr. Sloan were introduced by the Chair of the Anthropology Department, Prof. Hector Lime.

Neither the doctor nor the engineer were gifted public speakers. They mumbled their way through details of where the device had been found and the process through which they had learned how to operate the thing. This should have been fascinating, but the two men managed to make it all seem very dull. They were the sort who could drain excitement out of any topic, sharing a gift for pedantry capable of anesthetizing a room full of people in record time.

The moment of the actual demonstration finally arrived. Mr. Sloan put on a pair of heavy canvas gloves and touched one end of the device. The clear quartz slid open. Sloan pressed a recessed button inside the exposed chamber and the band of flexible metal began to move between the rollers.

We leaned forward as Sloan and Prescott stepped back from the table.

Silence. A silence that, though brief, seemed to stretch the room to an unbearable state of suspense.

Then a sound. Louder than any of us had anticipated, although why we should be surprised by the volume I do not know.

The sound was a low, rumbling burble. Having seen the mouth of a Martian in one of the museum's specimen cases, I can imagine it to be the orifice capable of emitting such a sound. It was initially hard to think of it as speech. It was a stream of low tones and a sort of cooing sound.

Then, sitting there in the lecture hall,

I suddenly felt my vision iris down within a reddish-brown circle as the blood left my brain and I feared I would pitch forward out of my seat in a dead faint.

I had heard this voice before.

Not exactly this voice, but something like it. A distortion of this speech. Garbled, filtered, and reproduced inexactly by a mouth not used to shaping itself around this alien language.

No. It wasn't possible. I must have been imagining things. The cumulative effect of the past year had taken a toll on my mind. Or so I told myself as I gripped the arms of my chair.

I had almost succeeded in convincing myself of this when the voice on the recording belt made a very particular sound. A sound I knew was a word.

I looked around at my fellow journalists. They were all leaning forward, listening intently, taking notes. But none of their faces reflected the dizziness I was experiencing.

The word surfaced in a different "sentence," then in a third. Each time as, what felt to me, a sort of desperate plea. I was engaged in a very real struggle to remain conscious and not tumble into the recorded voice's perceived despair.

A moment of terrible mental isolation came over me, and when it had passed I looked around the lecture hall and found I was sitting alone. The machine had been silenced. My colleagues were on stage with Sloan and Prescott, peppering them with questions. The two men appeared to be simultaneously thrilled by and leery of this attention.

I took the opportunity to leave the lecture hall unnoticed.

•

I found much of the street where Mr. Bosco lived had been smashed in the invasion. Whoever makes these decisions had looked at the neighborhood and found it undeserving of resurrection. But Mr. Bosco's building had escaped. It stood, alone, surrounded by rubble, stalwart and sturdy, like a last remaining guard at his post.

Mr. Bosco was still in residence. I found him in the same third-floor apartment. The inside of the apartment was as I remembered it, except there was the sense that the space and the building around it if not destroyed had been buffeted and shaken by the attack and now held itself and its contents with a tentativeness. There was a faint tremor to the place. As if the building had suffered a stroke.

Mr. Bosco was thinner, more deliberate in his movements. Mrs. Bosco had been killed in the early days of the invasion, but the girl who sliced the potatoes was still there, still looking after her uncle. She was, of course, older, but she did not seem to have matured beyond the point she had achieved when I first met her. She had physically aged, but the trauma of the invasion seemed to have arrested her emotionally. She appeared to me as a child being carried forward by a young woman's body.

I began to reintroduce myself to Mr. Bosco, but he remembered me as part of those last moments before the invasion. He remembered the difficulty with his device that day. The apparatus had survived the battles and was used now almost exclusively by Mr. Bosco as a means of communicating with his dead wife in the Thanasphere.

It was the Thanasphere I had come to speak with him about.

What would happen, I asked him, if some object from outside the Earth's orbit penetrated the Thanasphere on its way to the planet's surface? What would happen if there were living creatures aboard said object as it tumbled out of space? Would the thoughts of those creatures be detectable to Mr. Bosco's device?

He considered the questions and concluded such communications would be theoretically possible.

Then I asked another, potentially more blasphemous question. The Martian dead. If they had souls, as we understand the term, where would those souls have migrated upon the destruction of their corporeal form?

We were in the parlor when I asked him this. The same dark drapes were drawn against the sunlight. The device containing the electrodes in their galvanic fluid rested on its silver tray on the table, an exotic centerpiece of glass and metal and hope.

Mr. Bosco reached for one of the two straps connected to the device and held it in his hand. Then he said, "They would be above us."

What followed was week after week of searching blindly through the Thanasphere, listening. I was so focused on the search for un-Earthly . . . or perhaps I should say "Non-Earthly" . . . voices that it was several days before I consciously recognized something I had been oblivious to. Mr. Bosco, who, like myself, spoke English exclusively, had no problem understanding and communicating with the souls of men and women from every nation and culture on Earth, regardless of their language.

There is, apparently, a universality of thought that supersedes the arbitrary borders we map out on this globe. A universality not restricted to the human soul. For on the twenty-seventh day we found Vvv. Or perhaps Vvv found us.

While the unintelligibility of the first burst of Martian voices could be explained by their coming from living creatures passing through the Thanasphere in their conveyance, Vvv was understandable to us because he had, at the point we contacted him, "shuffled off this mortal coil."

What initially struck Mr. Bosco and myself was Vvv's regret for his race's attempted conquest. That was our first indication that while we knew something of Martian behavior, we had little sense of who they were.

So, we listened to Vvv. He told us his story in great earnest.

At first, I was alone taking notes during the sessions. It soon became clear that my hasty jottings would not be sufficient. I am therefore profoundly grateful to Miss Beatrice Havenhirst, Miss Sasha Goldstein, and Mrs. Olive Dunkerfield for their mastery of all things stenographic and typographical. Without them, this volume would not exist. A book that, in all honesty, is more transcription than translation.

With the manuscript complete I faced a question I'd been avoiding since the communications with Vvv began: If I were to make Vvv's account public, what would be the damage done to the world from learning the true nature of our invaders?

How would mankind react to the knowledge that so many people had been murdered by nincompoops and bureaucrats? That our parents and children, our husbands and wives were incinerated and poisoned by frightened conscripts thrown into battle by a leadership possessing less strategic skill than that of the manager of an average dry goods store.

What becomes of our stoicism then?

And what about the arguably far more disturbing adumbration, if Vvv's dying vision is accurate, that we owe our stewardship of this planet to colonization by an alien race countless eons ago? In which case, the dog currently sleeping and snoring on the floor next to me as I write this has a more legitimate claim to the title "indigenous species" than I do.

I did not expect the general public to be especially pleased and certainly not comforted by these revelations. As the source, if not the author, of this particular chronicle, I expected to be the target of any critical brick-tossing. In the end I decided any reputational discomfort I might suffer would be outweighed by knowing I had not concealed the truth.

Assuming you believe what you've read is the truth.
I must leave it to you. Believe Vvv's story or chalk it up to Mr. Bosco being an even more gifted humbug than I would have thought possible.

But even if you consider Mr. Bosco a crank and a fraud, and, by association, me along with him, there's one thing you still need to reckon with:
The word I heard from the Martian spool that day in the Museum, the word that sent me back to Vinegar Hill and Mr. Bosco. I'd heard the word once before. Only once. It was the word Mr. Bosco spoke before the Martians descended upon us after that last calm day in Brooklyn. The word that came to him through his device from the Thanasphere. A word no one had yet to hear on Earth.

The word, the name: YLLA.

Mr. J. G. Dougherty, Jr.
New York City, New York
December 31, 1900

—ABOUT THE AUTHOR—

JOSEPH DOUGHERTY is an Emmy and Humanitas Prize winner for his writing on the groundbreaking series *thirtysomething*. His movies include the Emmy-winning occult-noir mash-up *Cast a Deadly Spell*, which was nominated for a Ray Bradbury Award by the Science Fiction and Fantasy Writers of America, and the revisionist remake of *Attack of the 50 Ft. Woman*. He has contributed as a writer, director, and producer to several television series, including *Judging Amy*, *Once and Again*, and *Pretty Little Liars*. He is the author of *A Screenwriter's Companion: Instruction, Opinion, Encouragement* and the upcoming sequel *A Writer Directs: Theory, Discovery, Process* both from Fayetteville Mafia Press.

Dougherty earned Drama Desk and Outer Critics Circle nominations for his play *Digby* produced by Manhattan Theatre Club. He wrote the libretto for the Tony-winning musical version of *My Favorite Year* presented at Lincoln Center. His play *Chester Bailey* premiered at the American Conservatory Theater in San Francisco, where it was selected as Outstanding World Premiere Play and Outstanding Production of a Play by the TBA Awards. *Chester Bailey* was subsequently produced by the Contemporary American Theater Festival, Barrington Stage Company, and opened in New York at The Irish Repertory Theatre.